The Torch
of Tangier

The Torch
of Tangier

Aileen G. Baron

Poisoned Pen Press

Copyright © 2006 by Aileen G. Baron

First U. S. Edition 2006

10 9 8 7 6 5 4 3 2 1

Library of Congress Catalog Card Number: 2005928757

ISBN: 1-59058-221-7

Poisoned Pen Press
6962 E. First Ave., Ste. 103
Scottsdale, AZ 85251
www.poisonedpenpress.com
info@poisonedpenpress.com

Printed in the United States of America

This one is for Caroline and Michael, for Matthew and Rachel and Gabrielle and Isaac, and for the memory of Joey

Acknowledgments

My thanks go to Dr. Abdelhay Moudden of the Center for Cross Cultural Learning in Rabat for guiding me around Morocco, and to Dr. Farah Cherif, also of the Center, for introducing me to the story of her great-grandmother, Emily Keane, Shareefa of Ouezzane, and to Thor Kuniholm and the staff of the American Legation for showing me around the Legation and making old copies of the *Tangier Gazette* available to me.

I would also like to thank David Baron for suggestions he made after reading the manuscript in rough form. A thousand thanks to Sally Scalzo, Cathy De Mayo, and Linda McFadden for suffering through the many drafts of the book, to Jessica Kaye for handling the legal niceties of the contract, and to Javier Perez for encouragement and promotion.

And of course, my deepest gratitude goes to Barbara Peters, editor par excellence, whose deft hand helped whip the manuscript into its final shape, and to Robert Rosenwald, publisher of Poisoned Pen Press.

Much of the material in the book was gleaned from Carleton Coon's account of his work in Tangier for the OSS, *A North African Story,* and the story of his excavation in the Caves of Hercules in *Seven Caves.* Further exposition of these excavations can be found in *The Paleolithic of Tangier, Morocco*, by Bruce Howe.

Chapter One

Lily threaded her way out of the medina—the old city of Tangier—past old men wearing long, hooded djelabas, their bodies bent over canes as they struggled up the hill, their backless slippers shuffling along the littered street.

At first she didn't notice the two Germans keeping to the shadows. She saw them as she made her way back to the El Minzah Hotel from the medina but thought nothing of it.

Something about the pair struck her as familiar. Especially the one in the striped shirt, his neck bound by a tightly buttoned white collar. His wispy hair, dyed red-brown, had long white roots framing a ruddy, pockmarked face so that his head seemed to be floating away. His shirt, streaked with sweat, puffed outward around his arms. He looked like a weather balloon.

His companion had a moustache that punctuated his lips like a cocked eyebrow. From time to time he scanned the street with bulging bright blue eyes.

She had seen them yesterday, arguing in German with a man who wore a camel's hair jacket and a cold face. The man ignored Herr Balloon and concentrated on Lily, his eyes narrowed, his lips taut.

It was his eyes, stark icy blue, that sent a shiver through Lily's soul.

Herr Balloon's arms flailed in anger, the veins in his neck strained while the man in the camel's hair jacket continued to watch Lily.

His companion hung back with an embarrassed smile.

"Gottverdammte," she had heard Herr Balloon shout as the man in the jacket walked away and Herr Balloon ran after him before they both disappeared in the swarming streets surrounding the Grand Socco.

The white city, bleached and frowsy in the sun, spread languid and lascivious between the Mediterranean and the Mountain. It reverberated with sounds of expatriates: Italians crooning love songs in the golden dusk; Spaniards, stern-faced and stiff-spined, barking orders; Germans with pink faces and bawdy leers, singing and swaying together over beer in sidewalk cafes; drugged Americans with blank eyes, mumbling as they rolled along the streets; British pensioners with loud voices and rotted teeth, nursing warm drinks, staring into space, complaining about the price of food; openly affectionate pairs of men with raucous laughter that seeped from seedy bars and echoed through alleys.

"They're all spies," Drury had said. "Every last one of them. Watch your back."

And everyone complained about the shortage of food because of the war, but did nothing.

The Germans in front of her passed the gardens outside the Mendoubia and the 17th-century cannons—still aimed at the harbor, still ready to repel raids by marauding pirates and the unconquerable Moors.

Everything else had changed since Lily arrived in Tangier over a year and a half ago, in early 1941. Tangier had ceased to be an International Zone; Spain had assumed control of the Zone after the fall of France. Colonel Yuste, head of the Tangier occupation forces, appointed himself Governor General of Tangier. He dismissed the Mendoub, the Moroccan sultan's representative in the International Zone.

Now, a Nazi flag fluttered over the Mendoubia.

And everywhere, the Spanish police strutted, menacing and arrogant. And Nazi agents—pompous, insolent—swarmed out of the woodwork like termites after the rain and scurried through the streets of Tangier for the honor of the Fatherland.

Last November, almost a year ago, slurries of mud flooded part of the Caves of Hercules where she had worked, making excavation impossible. The archaeological team had to stop digging, waiting in the city until after the rain.

Then came Pearl Harbor.

The Spanish governors denied Americans access to Cape Spartel. We should have gone home, Lily thought, back to Chicago. Now it's the end of October, and we haven't been able to get back to the caves.

But Drury seemed to be waiting for something. They remained in Tangier, along with the other two members of the expedition staff, Clark MacAlistair and Zaid Sutton. The pair had flown here on the Pan-American Clipper with Drury before Lily arrived and stayed in a villa on the Mountain.

Drury paid for it all. He had money that seemed to fall out of the sky.

Lily skirted the dark shade of the huge banyan tree near the Mendoubia garden, its aerial roots anchored on the ground like the buttresses of a gothic cathedral.

The Germans were still ahead of her. Who were they? Refugees? Smugglers?

She passed Berber women in their conical straw hats and striped skirts, crouched next to sacks of saffron, cumin, and thyme. The musty odor of melons, over-ripe fruit, wine-heavy grapes, the bright tang of tangerines, hovered in the air. Women in dark robes, black veils stretched across their faces, floated past her.

The two Germans skulked ahead of her onto the Rue de Statut and toward the El Minzah. Were they spies? Would they work for whoever would pay them? Or were they Nazis?

Lily trailed them into the hotel. What were these two doing in the El Minzah? She could afford to stay there only because Drury paid her full room and board and gave her a small stipend.

The Germans prowled the reception area and descended the steps to the tiled patio where two tweedy Englishwomen sat by the fountain, noisily drinking Scotch and grumbling about prices.

"For the glory of the Empire," one of them bellowed in a resonant alto.

"Before the war," her companion said, "it cost less than four pounds a week here with full board. Full board, mind you."

"And what are you doing for the war effort?" her friend asked.

"Drinking the King's whiskey," said the woman. "Paying my bills as best I can. Had to give up food, you know. Too damned expensive."

Lily followed the Germans through the Wine Bar. Herr Balloon brushed against a woman who had been cooing at a toy poodle, feeding it bits of pretzel from a dish on the table. The poodle, wearing a pink bow and a rhinestone collar, snapped and growled in a high-pitched yelp as soon as Herr Balloon and his companion entered the bar.

The woman lifted the dog with her left hand and tucked it under her arm. *"C'est tout bien, mon petit chou,"* she crooned to the dog. *"Reste-toi tranquille, mon cher."*

"Entschuldigen." Herr Balloon gripped the woman's free hand and bowed over it. *"Pardon, Madame, perdón."*

Lily saw him slip a small piece of paper into her palm when he bent over.

"Crétin, idiot." The woman snatched her hand away, tucked the paper into the dog's collar, and waved the German off. "Go away, *barra. Allez-vous en!"*

Herr Balloon mopped his forehead with a dingy handkerchief, continued through the bar and up the stairs.

Lily followed at a distance to the first floor, watching the men slink through the corridor, moving out of sight when they paused. She ducked behind a writing desk that stood against the wall and saw Herr Moustache pull a passkey from his pocket, jiggle open a door, and creep inside.

Into Lily's room.

Chapter Two

Lily heard the clang of the elevator behind her, heard it hiccup to a level stop, heard the door open. She flattened herself against the wall and craned her neck to see the elevator.

Drury trudged out, frowning at some secret thought, a sheaf of papers tucked under his arm. He glanced up, noticed Lily, and raised an eyebrow. "What in hell are you doing hiding behind a potted palm?"

"Someone's in my room."

"What are you talking about?"

"Two Germans. They let themselves in with a key."

"They did, did they?" His lips formed into the bow of a smile, his eyes steely cold. "We'll fix that." He reached into his pocket for his room key. "We'll wait in my room 'til they're gone. Shouldn't take them more than ten minutes."

"I don't know what they're after. I have nothing of value."

"Course not." Drury signaled her inside and picked up the telephone. "Room service."

"You're not calling the police?"

"What police? Franco's boys, the Guardia Civil? They probably set this up. Did the same thing to me yesterday." He slapped the sheaf of papers down on the table next to him and waved Lily to a chair.

"You hungry?" He turned back to the telephone. "Dr. Drury here, room 114. An order of mashed potatoes, rolls with butter and honey, and a pot of tea. Immediately. *Directemente.*"

He crossed to the chair near the window and sat down. The bright sun behind him outlined his gaunt form in sharp contrast. "Saw Tariq in the Grand Socco yesterday, came in to tell me the Spanish army is occupying the caves. You know the High Cave where we found the Neanderthal? They use it as a stable for mules. Put anti-aircraft batteries on the headlands, right on top of the caves. Every time they shoot, a chunk of rock breaks off the roof of the cave. Practicing to shoot at *our* planes, I might add. Naturally, I complained to the Spanish authorities."

Naturally.

◇◇◇

Lily remembered the first time she had seen the caves, a few months after she had met Professor Hammond Drury that dark Chicago afternoon in the late fall of 1940 and agreed to come to Tangier. She sat in his office in Harper Hall at the University of Chicago, pretending he had said nothing to insult her, nothing to make her cringe.

He lounged in the chair, an expression of benign disdain in his cheerful smile.

A poster on the wall behind him pictured a kitten in front of a mirror. Looking back at it was the image of a valorous lion. The legend said, "What matters most is how you see yourself."

Lily gazed at his pointed features, his sharp chin, his wild white hair. Does he, too, see a lion in the mirror? A tiger? A kitten?

He had just told her she was not his first choice. "In fact," he had said, "I don't know if you're up to the job."

Women never are, she thought. Good archaeologists have short hair, need shaves, and climb cliffs in the morning before breakfast.

Until the day she sat in his office, she had worked on her dissertation every afternoon from 3:00 to 6:00 in her cubbyhole of an office at the Oriental Institute, site reports scattered on the floor, papers piled on the side of the desk. She had tacked a plan of Tel el Kharub—the site where she dug in Palestine—on the wall in front of her. Little pieces of paper stuck out from books stacked on chairs and bookshelves, marking pages she needed for reference.

Monday, Wednesday, and Friday mornings, she led discussion sessions for freshman classes in archaeology. Tuesdays and Thursdays, she had office hours. On Monday and Thursday evenings, before the war in Europe began, before Rafi left, they would have dinner together. Sometimes they went back to his apartment afterward and nestled in each other's arms.

Lily longed to break away from the wearying routine, go back into the field, to the blue sky and exotic faces, the excitement of strange streets. But most of all, she missed Rafi through the dreary days.

"They tell me you have some background with burials," Drury continued. "My own graduate students are great in the lab."

Of course they are.

"But they don't have much digging experience," he added. Then, that unctuous smile again.

She could see the falling snow through the tiny panes of glass of the mullioned windows behind him, the gunmetal Chicago sky, and the darkening outline of the Rosenwald Museum across the Midway.

"Morocco, Miss Sampson. The Magrebh."

That's where Rafi is, Lily thought. Rafi had returned to Palestine where they had met, this time to fight the Nazis. In his last letter, he said that he was with the British, somewhere in the Western Desert.

"The Magrebh," she repeated.

"Means west. All of North Africa west of Egypt is the Magrebh. Morocco is the westernmost of all. I leave in two weeks."

To be out of the snow and under the blue sky again. Can I be ready in two weeks? Can I leave my dissertation and the notes on Tel el Kharub behind, get back to them next year when I return? Why not? Some archaeologists take years to write reports, keep going back to the field.

"There's a war on," she said.

"We're not in the war yet, Miss Sampson. I booked your passage on the *Narragansett*. Leaves next month. Nothing to worry about, American registry. An old boat, not very fast. You'll be getting in sometime in January, in 1941. You'll have plenty of time to read up on the prehistory of Morocco during the crossing."

"Morocco is a French colony, Dr. Drury. Run by the Vichy government."

"Not to worry. Tangier's an international city."

"I don't know if I have the time. I haven't finished my dissertation."

Work, work, work. I'm sick of work.

"You won't need your doctorate. I'll make the crucial decisions."

Of course you will.

"Just competence in digging," he said. "That's all I ask."

"It's a Paleolithic site?"

"A cave."

"I'll think about it. Have to get back to the Oriental Institute."

When would she have to turn in her section of the site report to Kate in London? No hurry. Kate was busy with Home Defense.

Lily stood. Her notebook fell to the floor and her notes splayed across the faded weave of a kilim, stiff with mud, that Drury used as a rug. She grabbed the notes, stuffed a wad of them into the pouch of her notebook, and shoved the rest into the pocket of her coat between her gloves and scarf while Drury watched.

"I have office hours," she said and backed out of the room.

At the door of the building, she pulled out her scarf and the notes fell again. She picked them up, crossed the quad and skirted the Botany Pond in the lowering winter dusk, headed for her room at International House.

She ran into Drury again the next day as she was coming out of the Co-op on Ellis Avenue.

"Made up your mind?" Frozen droplets of breath billowed from his mouth. He shivered at the wind coming off the lake.

His leather-like skin, creased from countless summers in the North African sun, shone glazed and purple in the painful Chicago chill.

Her toes pinched with cold. She stamped her feet and felt the warmth evaporating through her muffler. "Warmer there than here?"

Frost hung on Drury's tangled eyebrows and on the edges of the fur hat that hid his thatch of white hair. "Start packing, Miss Sampson," he had said with one of those smug grins.

If he smiles in the wind, Lily had thought, his face will crack and his nose will fall off.

By the time Lily arrived in Tangier, the three of them—Drury, MacAlistair, and Zaid—had been working in the caves for the better part of a week.

The morning Lily joined them, MacAlistair and his friend Zaid were waiting for Lily and Drury in the patio of the El Minzah.

Zaid wore his digging outfit, his version of the local Riffian costume—loose pants in bright yellow, an embroidered vest, and a turban wrapped around his head for protection in the caves.

MacAlistair's jacket was draped across his shoulders and he held his cigarette European-style between his thumb and index finger. Nobody called him Mac.

He smoked Gauloise. The acrid whiff of the strong Turkish tobacco burned Lily's eyes. MacAlistair greeted them and coughed softly. His friend Zaid placed a hand on his arm.

"I shouldn't dig in the caves," MacAlistair said. "The dust is bad for my bronchitis."

He took another puff of the cigarette, coughed again until his eyes teared, while Zaid patted his back.

"Let's go," Drury said. "Time's a-wasting."

Zaid drove them out of Tangier in MacAlistair's Hillman, up a winding road lined with prickly pears and fragrant with the scent of wild iris. They started up The Mountain, strewn with villas silent behind walls festooned with ivy-geraniums and gardens vivid with spring.

Higher still along the ridge, the aroma of pine needles and the sea wafted toward them from round-headed umbrella pines along the coast. On their left, wild oleander bloomed bright pink among scattered cork oaks and in the crevasses of the scrub. Beyond, the Rif Mountains rose like ghosts out of a blue haze of rolling foothills.

They passed the lighthouse, sited on the barren point of Cape Spartel. In the distance children ran toward a low-lying kiosk on the edge of the land, their mothers following in wind-swept dresses.

Drury pointed to the flat, bald headlands of Cape Ashagar ahead of them on the coastal road. "There they are, on the Atlantic side of the cape." He paused dramatically. "The Caves of Hercules."

Parked cars, carriages, and donkey carts clogged the road near the caves.

"Who are all those people?" Lily asked.

"Tourists. Visitors. In good weather they drive out from town for picnics and sightseeing. And locals have an industry hewing millstones out of the walls of the sandstone caves. The only thing that bothers us is the noise of quarrying." Drury leaned forward and looked out the window toward the crowded road. "We work in the High Cave. It's a bear to reach, so tourists leave us alone."

Zaid maneuvered the car onto a spur that led to an upper path, and parked next to the cliff face in the shelter of a small niche not visible from the road. They unwound themselves from the tiny Hillman and stood in the freshening breeze that funneled through the Straits of Gibraltar.

The Pillars of Hercules!

From here, Lily thought, I can see the end of the world. Below them, the Atlantic roiled, green and foaming. Far to the right, inside the Straits, a turquoise Mediterranean reflected the sharp cerulean sky.

A blue-eyed Riffian with a blond beard and wearing a knitted cap, orange pantaloons, and a broad smile came toward them.

"This is Tariq," Drury said. "He's from the village down in the valley. Medionna. He and his brother Hasan are our pickmen."

Tariq touched his forehead and waved his hand in her direction. "Welcome, lalla, welcome."

They scrambled down a steep path that jutted from the cliff face like a tiny shelf, just broad enough for a footing, to the mouth of the cave. Here and there, the jagged ledge was shattered. Below her, the furious sea broke against the jumble of rocks. Lily held her breath and clawed the sharp limestone of the wall.

"Afraid of heights?" Zaid reached for her. "Take my hand." He guided her across the gaps to the entrance platform of the cave.

Inside, lit by a dim shaft of daylight from a hole in the roof, a series of strings one meter apart stretched across the floor. Lines weighted with plumb bobs hung from the ceiling like so many stalactites.

"Watch your step," Drury said, and handed her a miner's helmet with a lamp attached to the crown.

The others, their helmets already lit, moved cautiously among the strings, stooping under the low ceiling of the cave, casting long shadows across the cyclopean beams of the lamps. Only Lily could stand upright.

Tariq worked his way steadily along a trench down the center of the floor that led from the threshold of the cave to the back wall. He dug with the sharp end of a *khaddum*, a double-headed pick, straddling the trench, chopping at a layer of gritty red soil. His brother Hasan carried away the loose soil in a two-handled basket to a tiny shelf outside the cave.

"The boys sift the dirt through a screen with a quarter-inch mesh." Drury's voice echoed through the hollows of the cave, over the sound of the sea and the muted hammering of workmen in other caves quarrying mortars out of the rock. "We've picked up a few teeth, cut bone—some splintered for the marrow—from this level. Mainly gazelle, wild bovine."

Tariq, crouched over the trench, looked up at Lily and grinned. "My brother Hasan and I, we find."

"We dig in twenty centimeter increments," Drury told Lily.

He picked up a pebble and pitched it at the top layer of soil on the side of the trench. Lily swung her headlamp around to light it. Near the surface, the deposit was dark and oily from human habitation.

"That top layer had some modern Islamic and Roman remains and Neolithic material. Last year we brought out polished stone axes, impressed pottery, sheep bones, tanged Capsian points."

Tariq was working in the packed red earth below it.

"The red soil of the next level is from the last pluvial of the Pleistocene," Drury said. "We've taken out Mousterian points, scrapers, a Neanderthal jaw."

Lily peered into the shadows and adjusted her headlamp. She could just make out a lens of charcoal and burnt earth.

A Neanderthal hearth.

Here, in these caves at the tip of the world, they had cooked their food, chided their children, buried their dead. Long before the Romans, before the Phoenicians, even before Hercules, voices echoed in hollows lit by dim fires and the caves held the smell of habitation.

What were they like, these gruff creatures with their bulbous noses, heavy brows, receding chins? Was their hair matted? And did they smile, did they hold each other, did they croon soft songs to their babies?

MacAlistair had begun to cough again, this time uncontrollably. He groped for the cave entrance. Outside, he leaned against the rock face, gasping.

Zaid waggled his light dolefully from side to side. "He's sick. Very sick."

Zaid had stepped outside to comfort MacAlistair and Drury had explained, "Can't seem to shake the bronchitis."

◇◇◇

Lily was still staring at the shuttered window of Drury's room, the bright North African sun silhouetting his angular body, when his voice broke into her thoughts.

"Where the hell is room service?"

He began pacing the hotel room as if it were a cage. "Those goons must have cleared out of your room by now." As he reached for the telephone, a knock sounded at the door.

"At last." Drury opened it. He turned away from the waiter and indicated the desk. "Put the tray down here."

He signed the check and stood in the middle of the room until the waiter's footsteps faded, then went to the door, opened it a crack and scanned the hall.

"All clear."

He picked up the tray and carried it into the hall, pausing in front of Lily's room. "Not a word when we get inside," he whispered and signaled for her to unlock her door.

She opened it, hesitating in the hall a moment. Everything seemed to be in order, as if intruders had never been there. The Germans had vanished.

Drury eased the tray onto the dresser in Lily's room and held a finger to his lips. He ran a hand under the table, got down on the floor and looked under the dresser, the bed, the chair, all the while motioning her to silence. He took the drawers out of the dresser, turned them upside down, dumping the contents on the bed, emptied the closet, and ran his hand along the closet walls.

He went into the bathroom and peered in the medicine cabinet, under the sink, under the lid of the toilet tank. He climbed up on the toilet seat and loosened the screws holding the air grate.

He focused on the inside of the shaft, nodded knowingly, and signaled to Lily to look up.

There, inside the airshaft, dangling from a wire, was a microphone.

Chapter Three

Drury clambered down from the toilet, fetched the tray from the dresser, and brought it into the bathroom. He placed it on the sink, climbed back on the toilet seat, then slathered a coating of honey along the wire and the microphone. He motioned for Lily to hand him the mashed potatoes. He packed the soft mess around the microphone with his fingers, squeezing each clump to make it adhere.

"That should do it," he said out loud while he washed his hands. "The only thing they'll get now is an earful of potatoes."

"Suppose they're not hungry?" Lily said. "Besides, the food will attract every rat in the harbor."

"Not to worry." He climbed back up and screwed the grill in place. "The grid keeps all the rats in the airshaft. Except for the ones in the room above." He tapped on the ceiling with his middle finger.

"Someone's up there listening?"

"Probably. Earphones glued to their heads, eager for every word."

Lily felt a spark of irritation. "Why? I have no secrets."

He climbed down and wiped his hands on a towel. "Not yet."

"But you have secrets, Dr. Drury?"

He strode into the other room. "Let's have the tea."

"You do, don't you?"

"Milk or sugar?"

"It's cold by now."

"Doesn't matter. It's good for you."

"Won't they be suspicious when they don't hear anything?" Lily asked.

"Ignore them. They're buffoons. Chocolate soldiers in a comic opera."

Buffoons or not, Lily felt her shoulders tense.

He reached for the tea. "But don't underestimate them." He took a quick sip and put down the cup. "Drink up. We've an appointment at the villa." He moved to the door and held it open for Lily. "Come on, we're late." He stopped, halfway into the corridor. "Don't forget to lock up."

"The horse is already stolen."

"If you don't lock the door, they'll know we spotted them."

Outside the hotel, the woman who called herself Suzannah was canvassing stray tourists at her usual place, her shining black hair luminous in the morning sun. Drury had told Lily that Suzannah was a prostitute who lived in the mellah, the Jewish quarter of the medina.

He nodded when they passed her. The costumed doorman in slippers, fez, and orange sash, his hand clasped firmly on Suzannah's flank, shooed her away, telling her to go back to the mellah and stay there.

Drury glanced at Suzannah with an almost imperceptible nod of his head and looked toward a café across the street from the hotel. Lily watched Suzannah swivel down the street in her high-heeled shoes, her dark satin hair flapping against her shoulders like the wings of an angel, and tried to remember where she had seen Suzannah before.

They took a taxi up The Mountain to the villa. Lily waited at the gate while Drury paid the driver.

"It's open," he said when he came around to the gateway and reached behind the lock to lift the latch.

They skirted a black Packard parked in the circular drive in front of the villa and entered the tiled vestibule, made their way around a blocking wall and a corridor and into the villa, a quixotic blend of British and Moorish styles.

Drury stalked across the chintz and mahogany sitting room, with its beaded lampshades and Kerman throw rugs. He strode into a courtyard garden where the soft aroma of orange blossoms and old French roses hovered, where bougainvillea spilled against a dazzle of brilliant tiles, each tile matched to its neighbor with mathematical precision, circles embedded in circles, blue and yellow and white in intricate harmony.

MacAlistair and a stranger were seated next to the fountain in the shade of the eastern wall of the garden with glasses of mint tea on a table between them. They both rose when Drury and Lily entered.

"Lily, this is my friend Wild Bill," Drury said.

"Hickok?"

"Donovan." Drury turned to his friend. "Lily Sampson. I told you about her."

Donovan was a small man in his late fifties with pale blue unblinking eyes. He wore a windbreaker, but his trousers looked like officer's pinks.

"Donovan has a job in Gibraltar," Drury said. "Comes over here every once in a while for a decent meal."

"I understand you worked in Palestine," Donovan said to Lily.

"Tel el Kharub."

"The place where that archaeologist who was killed worked?"

Lily nodded. "Geoffrey Eastbourne."

"You're going back to finish the dig?"

"We closed down the site after Eastbourne was killed."

"What happens now?"

"His assistant, Kate Hale, is writing up the site report in London. I'm doing the section on the cemetery."

"You're working on it now?"

"I didn't bring my notes. I thought we'd just be here for the 1941 season, then go back to Chicago."

Donovan glanced at Drury. "But you stayed," he said to Lily. "Over a year longer. It's 1942, almost November now."

"The war," MacAlistair said. "How would she get home? She'd have to go south to the Cape, then over to South America."

"And Drury won't pay for that, I suppose." Donavan turned to Lily. "So what do you do with your time?"

"Not much. Getting to know the city."

"Participant observation. Isn't that what you anthropologists call it?"

"I'm an archaeologist. I'm just observing, not participating." Again Donovan glanced at Drury.

"You speak Arabic, Miss Sampson? French or Spanish?"

"I can speak a little of the local dialect they use in Palestine. It's different from what they use here but I can understand most of what the Tanginos are saying. As for French, my pronunciation is awful and my vocabulary tends toward archaeological terms like *tesson* for potsherd, *niveau* for level. Just high school Spanish."

"But you can get along."

"Pretty much."

"With all that free time, you must be bored. Maybe you could help out at the Legation."

"I don't..." Lily began.

But before she was sure of her answer, Drury stepped in. "Great idea. We'll both go down there, offer our services."

Donovan gave a grunt of approval. He moved toward the door. "I took the liberty of mentioning both of you to the chargé d'affaires at the Legation. Name is Quentin Boyle. He's expecting you."

Drury seemed satisfied. "We'll drop by this afternoon."

"I'll call and tell him you're coming." Donovan started to leave. "Be careful," he said to Drury and then turned to Lily. "Good to have met you Miss Sampson. Maybe we'll meet again." He sauntered toward the inside of the house and then stepped back into the garden.

"While you're there," he said to Drury, "check out the personnel. I'd like to hear what they're up to."

"Something wrong?"

"Nothing I can put my finger on."

MacAlistair coughed gently, looking from Donovan to Drury and back to Donovan. "I'll see you out," he said and followed Donovan out of the garden.

"Looks like you'll be working at the Legation," Drury told Lily.

"How do you know? We haven't gone there yet, haven't asked for the job."

"Wild Bill always gets his way. Nobody can turn him down."

MacAlistair returned, followed by Zaid.

"Who was that?" Zaid asked.

MacAlistair hesitated, looked over at Drury. "A friend of Drury's."

"What was he doing here?"

"Dropped by to say hello," Drury said.

Lily watched the water splay in the fountain while MacAlistair crossed to the chair he had been sitting in earlier, sat down with a sigh, and picked up the glass of tea.

Zaid sat in the other chair and leaned forward. "The tea is cold. I'll get you a fresh pot."

"We have to leave. Have an appointment at the Legation," Drury told him.

Zaid seemed annoyed, distracted. "Want me to drive you?" He stood up, searched in his pocket and pulled out the car keys.

"Sure." Drury strode out of the garden, through the sitting room, and was waiting at the Hillman before Zaid and Lily reached the drive outside the gate.

Chapter Four

At the Legation, the acrid smell of an old building—damp plaster and musty wood—hung in the air. A Marine corporal in dress uniform perched in a glass enclosure at the entrance nodded to Drury and gave Lily a quizzical look.   .

"She's with me," Drury told him. "We have an appointment with Boyle."

The corporal waved them through.

<><><>

In the office of the chargé d'affaires, Quentin Boyle leaned back in his chair, both hands on his desk. "So you say you're an expert on Arab affairs, know how they think."

Boyle had auburn hair and a pale redhead's skin. He had a nick on the right side of his nose, and his nostril flared and fluttered when he spoke.

Drury sat on the edge of his chair. "I know the Riffians," he repeated, his tone growing more insistent with each sentence. He leaned his elbow on Boyle's desk. "Came here in the Twenties during the Riff war when they fought for their independence against Spain. Fascinating people. Blue-eyed, blond Arabs." He gave Boyle a knowing grin. "The Vikings were great explorers."

"You're trying to tell me Leif Erikson was here?" Boyle glanced at Lily with half a smile, as if expecting a reaction. She raised an eyebrow and Boyle glared at Drury's arm resting on the corner of his desk.

He removed his glasses and leaned forward. "This is the second time you walked into my office to make demands and tell me what to do. And now you have your friend Donovan call, put the pressure on me." Boyle waved his glasses in Lily's direction. "And Goldilocks over here? What does she want?"

Goldilocks?

"She's my assistant," Drury said.

"I'll bet she is."

"My name is Lily Sampson." Goldilocks, indeed. "But you may call me Miss Sampson. I'm an archaeologist. I've worked on sites in the Middle East before."

"This isn't an excavation, Miss Sampson. And we aren't in the Middle East," Boyle said. "The Middle East is the Levant, Palestine, Syria. This is the Near East."

Drury let out an impatient sigh. "I know the founder of the Republic of the Riff, Abd el-Krim."

Boyle drummed his fingers, his gaze fastened on Drury's hands resting next to the tray of pens on Boyle's desk. "I don't know what you're really after." He watched as Drury rearranged the pens in the tray. "I know you're up to some tricks, but I don't know what they are. I only know that I have instructions from higher up to accommodate Donovan." Boyle's nostrils expanded with an irritated quiver and a pink flush of anger suffused his face. "And frankly, I resent it. I wouldn't know what to do with you. You don't know squat about consular work."

He looked pointedly at Drury's hands, still fumbling with the pens on Boyle's desk.

"I apologize for whatever." Drury dropped his hands to his lap and leaned back in the chair. "Didn't mean to step on your toes, but I'm here to help. There's a war on, you know."

With a contemplative nod, Boyle twirled his glasses by the earpiece, first clockwise, then counterclockwise. "We're in a delicate situation here. Have to be careful. It's touch and go whether Franco will join the Axis."

"I understand." Drury bent toward Boyle again and lowered his voice. "That's where the Riffians come in." He spoke slowly now. "We can use them in a pinch, throw them against the Kraut. I'm sure of that."

Boyle took in his breath. He seemed to give the suggestion some thought, nodding his head, tapping his fingers, blowing out his cheeks. "At the least Spain may allow German troops free passage through the territory."

Boyle fiddled with the paper clips in the well of the pen tray. "Maybe there is something you can do. Let me talk to Armand Korian." He folded his glasses, placed them on the desk, and strode to the door. He signaled the secretary. "Tell Korian to bring the news bulletins."

He returned to the desk, the door still open. "Korian edits the Legation Bulletin," he told Drury. "We send out pamphlets in French, Spanish, Arabic." He shrugged. "Doesn't seem to do much good."

"Miss Sampson can be of some help," Drury said. "She's supposed to be working for the State Department, like me."

That's the first I've heard of it, Lily thought.

Boyle raised his eyebrows. "You work for State?"

Drury nodded and leaned forward again. "You have an empty room here she can use? She can sit, read books. She won't bother you. She'll keep out of your way."

Out of his way? Nothing like feeling superfluous.

Boyle shook his head. "We don't have room here." He looked Lily up and down with an appreciative smile. "Why don't you spend your time at the beach, Miss…?"

"Sampson." My God, is he flirting? Should I bat my blue eyes? Fluff out my golden hair?

"She needs a cover. For safety," Drury said.

"I'm busy serving the government here. Proud of it, I might add." Boyle hesitated, then continued in a more conciliatory tone. "So are you, I suppose, in your way. And from what I can see of your friend, Miss…?" He paused.

Lily sat straighter in the chair. "Sampson," she repeated.

"Miss Sampson." Boyle looked her up and down again. "You've got nothing to be ashamed of, either." Boyle smiled at her. "Go to the beach."

Drury rose, blocking Boyle's affable leer. "She'll be too noticeable there."

Boyle tilted back his chair. "Indeed she will."

The secretary knocked on the open door. "Korian is here with the pamphlets."

Boyle brought his chair upright. "Go to the beach, Miss Sampson. Improve our relations with the Tanginos."

A man came into the office, clutching a pipe between his teeth. He carried a stack of leaflets and balanced them on the edge of Boyle's desk.

"Meet Armand Korian," Boyle said. "He's in charge of our news bulletin. Counteracts Spanish propaganda."

Korian had droopy eyes, a sharp nose, and hair glowing with too much brilliantine. He wore a shiny three-piece suit with baggy pockets and a blue spotted bow tie. He looked like an unsuccessful insurance salesman.

The front of his shirt and his lapels were dappled with bits of tobacco and ash. He reached into a pocket and pulled out a pouch of pipe tobacco.

"Professor Drury here is an expert on the region," Boyle told Korian.

Korian looked at Drury and waggled the pipe in his mouth.

"He's going to assist you with the bulletin."

Korian began to fill his pipe. "I don't need any help."

Boyle handed a leaflet printed in Arabic to Drury. "Read this, tell us what you think of it."

Korian pulled a match from his pocket and lit it by scraping his thumbnail across the head while Drury stared at the leaflet in his hand. Korian began to draw on the pipe and Drury crossed to the window, held the paper to the light and squinted at it.

Boyle waited. Korian puffed, billowing smoke out of the side of his mouth. The room filled with the sticky-sweet smell of his pipe tobacco.

"Trouble reading it?" Korian took the pipe from his mouth and aimed the stem at Drury. "Need some help?"

Drury brought the paper closer, then held it at arm's length and stared at it.

Boyle picked up a pencil and tapped it on the desk. "I thought you knew Arabic."

"Haven't studied classical, printed Arabic in years. It's worthless here, you know. The farther you get from Syria, the less it's understood."

Korian took a draft of his pipe. "How do you manage, then?" He let out a smoke filled breath.

"With locals, I speak Mogrebhi, the local Arabic. Stick to simple subjects." Drury waved the smoke away and gave a measured cough. "Why aren't you in the army?"

"Punctured ear drum. And it's none of your business," Korian took a deep draw on the pipe and blew another cloud toward Drury. "The locals understand Arabic."

"Just Moroccan Arabic. Mogrebhi." Drury pushed away the smoke like a swimmer stroking through surf. "Berbers speak a local language, Tamazight. Almost a third of the population here are Jews and they use a different dialect—mixture of medieval Spanish and Hebrew. They brought it from Spain during the Inquisition. Call it Ladino."

Korian looked sleepy, with bags under his eyes so heavy they looked like they could fall from their own weight. "I understand the people here," he said through a haze of smoke.

"You don't know which side they butter their bread," Drury told him.

"My family is from Lebanon." He shrugged and flicked a speck of tobacco from his lapel. "I'm an Arab, more or less."

"I'd say less. You don't know the locals." Drury looked Korian over, lingering on the stains on his lapel and his over-polished shoes. "You're not an Arab, you're Armenian, born and raised in California, in the Central Valley."

Drury began to pace the area in front of the desk, his hands clasped behind his back. He shook his finger at Korian as if to a naughty child. "And it's time you had a short course on Moroccans and their languages." He cleared his throat and folded his arms. "The Romans called them Mauri, derived from the Hebrew word for west, but the Berbers were the indigenous 'Libyans' of North Africa. They've been here since the dawn of history, known to the Egyptians as 'Lebu.'" Striding up and down as if he were in a lecture hall, he droned, "The Riffian dialect changes Arabic 'L' to 'R'. 'F' and 'B' are interchangeable, hence Rifi from Libi."

Korian rolled his eyes to the ceiling. "We have to listen to this?"

Boyle grunted and Drury resumed pacing.

"I'm giving you the benefit of fifteen years of education and research."

Once he gets started, there's no stopping him, Lily thought. He'll harangue us forever. She picked up a bulletin.

"You read Arabic, Miss Sampson?" Boyle broke in.

"I read it but don't speak it. It says here that Doolittle led an air raid on Tokyo."

Korian gathered the pamphlets. "That's what it says. Good for you."

He eyed Drury disdainfully and stalked out of the room, wafting tobacco smoke behind him.

Boyle closed the door after him. "One thing I'd like you to tell me is how you know the background of Legation personnel." He waited. "You won't say, of course."

Boyle looked from Lily to Drury and back again. "You're anthropologists, aren't you?"

Drury finally stopped pacing. "That's what we are."

"You know how people in foreign cultures think?"

"That's what we do for a living."

Boyle folded his glasses and held them in his hand. "Wouldn't hurt if you prepared a report on the Riff. Work up a pamphlet about propaganda in Morocco, what would work, what wouldn't."

"Exactly what I had in mind."

Boyle tapped his glasses against his hand. "Can't pay you, of course."

"Wouldn't take the money if you could." Drury sat in the chair facing Boyle's desk and leaned back luxuriantly.

"It's settled then," Boyle said. "Busy yourself with Arab affairs, find out what they're thinking, how they can be influenced."

"We'll both work on it." Drury looked over at Lily. "As a team. Just want to do our bit for the war effort."

"And you'll shut up and leave me alone." Boyle opened the door for them. "God help us. With teams like this, we could lose the war."

Lily saved her comments until they were back on the Rue de Statut.

"Boyle made me feel like a floozy."

"He meant it as a compliment. Forget it."

"Why'd you tell them we could do a pamphlet on propaganda?"

"We can. We'll do an ethnography, chapters on social organization, kinship terms, religion. Contrast tribal areas with cities."

"I don't know enough about the Berbers."

"Doesn't matter. Throw in some anthropological jargon. Makes a good impression. The more ponderous and mysterious, the greater they'll think it is."

While he was talking, Drury stared across the street. Lily followed his gaze. Suzannah was seated at a sidewalk table in a café across from El Minzah. When they passed, Suzannah raised her eyebrows then looked away.

"Besides," Drury said, his voice hesitant, distracted. He was still looking in Suzannah's direction. "They think I work for the COI, Coordinator of Information, doing research and propaganda."

"Don't you? Who do you work for?"

Drury peered at Lily and then glanced across the street. Suzannah picked up a glass and held it to her lips without drinking.

Lily was certain Drury had given Suzannah a hidden signal, but what the signal was, or why he sent it to her, Lily couldn't tell.

"Who is she, really?" Lily asked.

Drury was watching Suzannah. "Who?" He smiled and gave Suzannah an almost imperceptible nod.

"Never mind," Lily said. She had remembered where she had seen Suzannah before.

Chapter Five

The first time Lily saw Suzannah was on Cape Spartel, outside the Caves of Hercules. Suzannah was a passenger in one of the taxis that had come from town on a sightseeing excursion to the caves.

It was a windy day, just after noon. Zaid had been sifting soil from the trench through a rocker screen on the apron of the cave, looking for small finds—teeth, bone fragments, pieces of debitage and small tools. That day he wore turquoise pantaloons and a red sash, his head wrapped with a bright yellow turban. A sudden gust came up from the Strait and blew a cloud of dust into Zaid's face.

He let out a howl and covered his eye.

MacAlistair ran out of the cave. "Don't rub it," MacAlistair called and rushed to Zaid. Tariq was ahead of him, already looking into Zaid's eye. Tariq rolled back the lid and licked the eyeball with his tongue.

"Stop that," MacAlistair shouted.

Tears from Zaid's reddened eye cut a track through the dust on his face as they streamed down his cheek. He clapped his handkerchief to his eye again.

"You need a doctor," MacAlistair said, and scanned the line of taxis parked on the path up to the caves. "Maybe one of the tourists can take you to town."

MacAlistair started down the path, wheezing slightly. Lily followed. Before he was halfway, he stopped, gasping, and leaned against the cliff face.

"Your asthma again," Zaid said. "Rest awhile."

Lily took MacAlistair's arm. "Asthma" was one of the euphemisms they tacitly agreed on. Sometimes it was "bronchitis," sometimes "your respiratory problem."

Zaid shook his head and grimaced. "We're a walking hospital."

The cloth clasped to his eye, Zaid started down the path alone and approached a taxi about to pull away. He addressed the French passengers, speaking in his best French, with only a slight North African accent. The woman passenger backed away and started to roll up the window.

Zaid told them he had suffered an accident, needed a ride back to town to see a doctor, and asked if he could share their taxi. He offered to pay.

The woman screamed. The man shook his fist and shouted, "Get away from her, you filthy Arab. *Va t'en*! Come any closer and I'll club you."

Zaid turned pale and clenched his fingers. Before he could answer, Suzannah stepped out of one of the parked taxis. A young Spaniard in the back seat tried to pull her back by her skirt.

"You will come with us, Zaid." Suzannah cooed at Zaid as if he were a bird. "We will carry you to a physician." The Spaniard shook his head in dismay.

Above them on the slope, the wind caught the pile of dust from the rocker screen and swirled it around. A paroxysm of coughing seized MacAlistair. His shoulders heaved.

Suzannah watched as MacAlistair covered his mouth with a handkerchief, drew it away and stared into it, his body convulsing for breath.

"I will carry you both to the physician," she said.

Zaid started back up the path. He reached for the trembling MacAlistair with his free hand, his other hand shielding his eye with the cloth.

"Step carefully," he said.

With Lily on one side of MacAlistair and Zaid on the other, they stumbled from boulder to boulder.

"Look at them," Suzannah said to the young Spaniard. "It is the blind leading the halt." The young man in the taxi gave a helpless shrug and sat back. "I must fetch my friends, *querido*," Suzannah said to the Spaniard. "*Espere aqui.* Stay here."

Suzannah reached for Zaid's arm. Two by two—Suzannah with Zaid and Lily with MacAlistair—the four of them made their way down the rocky path to the waiting taxi.

"We will pay," Lily had heard Zaid say before he climbed into the back seat.

"Indeed you will," Suzannah had answered.

That evening, amid the arabesques and lilies in the courtyard of the villa, Zaid had hunkered in his chair, his eye covered by an enormous bandage, his head resting on his hand. He had muttered and growled, still rankling with the insult from the French in the taxi.

"I should have killed them. Ignorant peasants. Who do they think they are?"

He touched the bandage gingerly and winced. "I am nobler than all the pashas and governors. I descend from kings and princes, the old Moors of Granada who ruled before it was lost to the Nazarenes."

MacAlistair laid a sympathetic hand on his arm.

"I am nobler than any Nazarene," Zaid told him. "Nobler than you, MacAlistair, with your British pretensions."

"Please, Zaid," MacAlistair had said. "Don't upset yourself. We all love you here."

"I'm only a bit of local color to you."

"That isn't fair, Zaid."

"You love me like you love a performing poodle. I'm your pet, with a jeweled collar, and I dance at the end of a golden chain."

Embarrassed, Lily had looked away and watched the water play in the blue tiled fountain in the middle of the courtyard garden.

But she never forgot Zaid's rancor.

Chapter Six

Herr Balloon or his companion seemed to hover outside the hotel entrance whenever Lily and Drury left for the Legation in the morning.

"They're nobody," Drury said when Lily looked over at them. "If they mattered, they'd be in Paris."

Lily and Drury would leave the hotel at nine o'clock and work at the Legation until about four. The Germans looked seedier and seedier each day. "They're monitoring your room on spec," Drury said to Lily. "Nobody's paying them. You can see that. I told you. Nothing to worry about."

Still, Drury looked back over his shoulder whenever the Germans followed.

When they reached the stairway that led to the Legation and crossed under the arch into the quiet maze of white-walled alleys, the Germans would stay behind, watching from the landing.

Lily and Drury shared a clammy, high-windowed office in the Legation, no bigger than an oversized broom closet, furnished with two desks and a bookcase. A bright Moroccan rug covered the worn glazed tiles.

The first chill of autumn seeped into the dank room.

"Can't the U.S. government afford a newer building?" Lily asked. "This smells like an old shoe."

"Have a little respect for history," Drury said. "This is the oldest American government building in the world."

"I wouldn't doubt it."

"Morocco recognized America in 1776, while the ink was still wet on the Declaration of Independence. First country that recognized us." An expansive wave of his arm wafted over their tiny office and included the hall outside. "This was once a sultan's palace, a gift to America from the Kingdom of Morocco."

They worked on the pamphlet every day, cobbling it together from books in the Legation library and from yellowed notes on brittle paper in trunks that Drury kept in storage in MacAlistair's villa.

Lily wrote about the cultural history of the zone; Drury, about physical characteristics and diseases of the indigenous population. Lily wrote about social organization, residence, and kinship; Drury, about language, resolution of conflict, and political organization.

The work went smoothly, except when Drury leaned over Lily's shoulder to see what she had written. Then the cramped office, the tight writing on the pages, the damp smell of the place bothered her.

One of those afternoons, when she felt restless and out of sorts, she decided to take a break.

She put down the pen and left the office, left the Legation and started to walk through the crowded streets of the medina, into the bustling fondouk market with its tangy aroma of spices, of apples, of half-rotted vegetables. She pushed her way past shoppers haggling with Berbers hawking produce heaped high on carts, past women squatting next to squares of cloth laid out on the sidewalk and piled with mounds of rice, of thyme, of cumin.

She noticed a Berber watching from the edge of the crowd. He's from the south, she thought, noting his dark skin, the reddish-brown stain of his teeth, his striped burnoose. He's from Marrakech, the Red City, where the iron-infused soil tinted the mud brick walls with a roseate glow and seeped into the well water to pit and stain the teeth of children.

She passed him and climbed up, up into the calm above the market, through cobbled lanes and alleys that snaked among the whitewashed walls of houses.

Over subdued street sounds—children's voices, mothers calling—she heard the shuffle of Berber slippers close behind her.

She looked back. It was the Berber from Marrakech she had seen in the fondouk market.

She paused at a café near a street corner, where men and women seated at outdoor tables nursed glasses of tea, browsed through newspapers, played at backgammon.

She took a table and ordered a mint tea. As she sipped it, she gazed down the street, watching women trudging with net bags stuffed with vegetables, watching strollers hiking up the hill.

When she saw the man with the camel's hair jacket at the corner, she felt a prick of anxiety. He was talking with the Berber. The man leaned against a wall, his head back, his eyes half closed. He was talking to the Berber but looking at Lily. What bothered Lily most was the man's eyes, the irises ringed in dark blue, the rest so light they were almost white. They were like ice.

The man stopped talking and ducked into an alley.

Lily paid for the tea and got ready to leave. She started down the hill toward the Legation.

Once more she heard the Berber's footsteps behind her.

Don't look back, she told herself, and felt a chill running up her spine.

She could feel him coming closer, felt his presence on the back of her neck.

She started to run and heard his footsteps slap against the cobbles, the sound of them faster and faster, closer and closer.

He caught up with her when they were out of sight of the café.

He grabbed her arm.

His face was blank, his eyes cold. "You will come with me."

There was no one else in sight.

"Why should I go with you? Who are you?"

His grip tightened.

"I don't know the city." Lily tried to pull away. "I can't give you directions." She felt his thumb pressing on the inside flesh of her arm. "You're hurting me."

"What do you do for Drury?"

"Drury?"

The pressure on her arm increased. A jolt of panic crept into her throat.

"I don't know what you're talking about."

He leaned into Lily, started to twist her arm.

Instinctively her knee jerked up and she jammed it into his groin.

He loosened his grip, began to double over.

His knitted cap fell to the ground.

A flurry on the edge of her peripheral vision made her glance to the side. Drury stood at the bottom of the street emerging from an alley, transfixed, waving his arms, his mouth opening and shutting, shouting, starting up the hill.

Her breath came in gasps and a surge of alarm pounded in her ears, fluttered in her eyes. She couldn't hear Drury.

The Berber reached for her again. She kicked at him, shoved him back with both hands.

He staggered, hit his head on the corner of the building, sank to his knees and collapsed onto the cobbles.

"You all right?" she heard Drury ask from behind her.

"He'll be all right, won't he?" Her voice caught. "I just pushed him." She was staring at the Berber lying motionless on the ground. "He was trying to…."

"I saw." Drury gave her an appraising look. "Remind me to keep my distance when your adrenaline is up. You have more talents than I suspected."

Drury bent down and felt the man's pulse.

"He's dead?"

"No." Drury looked up at Lily. "He'll live."

Drury felt along the Berber's head. Flakes of whitewash from the building dropped out of his hair. "He has a concussion."

"Who is he?" Lily asked.

"I'm not sure."

Drury patted the man's body, turned him over and felt under the burnoose. He pulled out a knife and then, a gun.

"A Luger." Drury rose. "Let's get out of here before he wakes up with a headache."

They hurried downhill through silent streets.

"You could have been killed," Drury said as they plunged back into the tangle of the fondouk market, before they lost themselves in the safety of the crowd and made their way back to the Legation.

That evening, Zaid was late for dinner. The three of them, Lily, Drury, and MacAlistair, waited for him, seated at the table in the courtyard of the villa.

"It's taken care of," Zaid said as he sat down, and Faridah, the cook brought out a steaming tureen.

None of them spoke until almost the end of the meal.

Lily broke the silence. "That Berber this morning," she said to Drury. "Why was he asking about you?"

Drury put down his fork. "Was he now?"

"He was talking to a man with steely eyes when I first saw him. The man gave me the creeps."

Zaid pushed his plate away and leaned back in his chair. "Your Berber was a dangerous man."

"What do you know about him?" she asked.

"His name was Saleem."

"Was?"

Zaid took a packet of Gauloise from his pocket. "He had an accident."

A surge of anguish flooded through her. "The concussion?"

"No, nothing like that," Drury said. "It happened much later in the day."

"How?"

"You had nothing to do with it." Zaid busied himself with opening the pack of cigarettes. "He slipped as he was getting into the bath. Drowned in the bathtub."

"You heard it on the news?"

Zaid shook a cigarette from the packet. He didn't look up. "Things like that are not reported in the news." He seemed to be smiling.

"The police, then?"

Lily looked across the table at Zaid. He took a box of matches from his pocket. "They don't know about it yet."

"Well then, how do you know?" She felt a sudden, inexplicable anger. "You killed him, didn't you? In cold blood." Her voice rose, trembling. "What's wrong with you? He was a simple Berber, for God's sake."

"He was a traitor, was willing to sell out Morocco to Europeans," Zaid said. "He worked for the Germans, worked for the French. For money."

"Zaid handles…" MacAlistair began, and looked over at Zaid.

He rolled the cigarette between his fingers and began tapping the end of it against the side of the box.

"Zaid," Drury said, "has contacts, knows people, knows how to get things done."

Lily waited for him to say more.

"The Berber worked for Gergo Ferencz," Drury added. "Ferencz runs German intelligence here in Tangier."

"You should be grateful to Zaid," MacAlistair told her. "The man threatened you, tried to kidnap you, could have killed you. Zaid handles problems like that, watches over us."

Zaid lit the cigarette. "I do what I can," he said and shrugged.

His tongue flicked at a piece of tobacco stuck on his lip and he rubbed it off with his finger.

"And he does it so well." MacAlistair beamed at him like a proud father.

Chapter Seven

Drury trudged back to their office with the mail, rifling through it as he came down the hall. He stopped once, examined one of the envelopes, turned it over, and glanced toward Lily at her desk.

"This came for you in my packet." He hesitated before handing it to Lily. "It's been traveling around awhile."

She stood up and reached for it. The envelope was smudged, re-addressed, and branded with forwarding stamps. The original address, in Rafi's handwriting, was International House at the University of Chicago. It had been forwarded to the Oriental Institute and sent from there to other addresses that Lily had never heard of. This was the first letter that she had received from Rafi in a year. It seemed a miracle that it had reached her.

"Who's it from?" Drury asked.

"I have a... friend."

"A friend?"

Lily felt her cheeks flush. "He's somewhere in the Maghrebh."

"He's British?"

"American. He's attached to the British."

Drury glanced at the letter poised in Lily's hand. "When's the last time you heard from him?"

"This is the first letter in a long time."

Drury reached out toward her, hesitated and drew his hand away. "Have some business down the hall. Be back in a while."

She waited until he was out of sight and his footsteps faded before she opened the letter.

"I have your picture in my tent," it began. *"It's the only thing that keeps me going. I look at you and think about when all this is over, when I come home and we are married. I kiss you before we sit down to dinner. Sometimes we have a Frank Lloyd Wright house in Oak Park; sometimes we already have two children. But always, I kiss you before dinner."*

Most of the letter was unreadable. The British military censors had made hash of the rest of the first page, blacking out phrases, whole lines, alternate words. The letter made no sense until well down on the second page.

"Stories are coming out of Europe about Nazi concentration camps, about evil too terrible to imagine, stories of slavery, stories of torture, of sadistic 'scientific' experiments on human beings that make the Inquisition sound like a picnic in the park. It's as if a whole nation has gone mad. We must win here in North Africa so that we can attack Europe and beat them back into oblivion. I will do anything to stop them. Anything."

She folded the letter and held it in her hand before returning it to the envelope. It had journeyed through time and space, was soft with wear; yet still seemed warm with his breath. She clung to it, clenching it in her skirt pocket, and felt the envelope curl within her hand.

She took it from her pocket again and ran her finger along the ragged edge of the envelope. The postmark read Tobruk, June 10, 1941. More than a year ago.

Fear washed over Lily as she thought of the battle in the Western Desert, the hasty retreat and evacuation, and finally the fall of Tobruk at the end of June.

She put the letter back in her pocket, patted it twice, sighed, and went back to work.

She settled herself at the desk, reached for the top paper on the stack, changed her mind, and then took Rafi's letter out of her pocket and weighed the envelope in her hand.

Tobruk, June 10.

She opened the letter again, expecting to find terrifying news hidden between the words. She held the first page, scarred with heavy black censor marks, up to the light to see if she could read what had been crossed out. Useless.

Tobruk in June. Lily put both arms on the desk to cradle her head as a feeling of dread crept over her.

"I have your picture in my tent," she read again. "Always, I kiss you before dinner." The words rang through her head like a tocsin.

He's all right. "He must be all right or I would have heard by now," she said aloud.

Get back to work.

Lily jammed the letter back into her pocket, flicked some imaginary dust off her skirt, and straightened herself in the chair.

She reached for the stack of papers again and began sorting them, putting them in order.

◇◇◇

Back in the office, Drury looked over Lily's shoulder to see what she was writing. She was rattled and gouged a line through the last sentence. He picked up the sheaf of foolscap she had stacked at the edge of the desk and thumbed through the manuscript. Each page read like a maze, interrupted with crossed-out lines, arrows that led from broken sentences and paragraphs, from carats to sentences written sideways in the margins.

He rotated the paper in his hand and crooked his head. "We need a secretary." He tossed the page onto her desk. "Come on."

Dragging Lily behind him, he marched into Boyle's office, demanding a secretary.

"Can't spare the personnel," Boyle told him.

"Hire someone," Drury said.

"Too complicated. They need security clearance. Can't hire just anyone."

When Drury showed up the next day with Suzannah in tow, Lily wondered how the Legation staff would react. "I'll vouch for her," Drury had said.

"Get out of my office." Boyle's voice reverberated down the corridor. Korian came out to the hall to watch the tableau.

"And take your doxie with you," Boyle shouted.

Korian backed out of Drury's way with a knowing glance and the shadow of a smile as Drury slammed down the hall back to his office.

"I should have punched him in the nose," Drury told MacAlistair that evening. They were all having dinner together at a restaurant in the medina, Drury and Lily, MacAlistair and Zaid.

"Suzannah's a prostitute, for God's sake," MacAlistair said.

"What do you know about Suzannah?"

"Very little." MacAlistair's breath caught and he coughed into a napkin. "What did you expect?"

"A little respect for my status," Drury said. "A little respect."

"What status? What does he know about you? What does he know about Suzannah?"

"Nothing." Drury picked up his wineglass, took a sip. "I can't—." He waved the glass in the air and put it down.

"Well, then," MacAlistair said.

"Nevertheless."

Chapter Eight

The next morning, Drury glowered at the German who waited in the shadow of the entrance to the hotel.

"Trying to wither him with a glance?" Lily asked.

Drury gave an exasperated grunt. "This has to stop," he said, loud enough to be heard by the German.

They started toward the medina and the German followed, pretending not to have heard. Drury took a tortuous route through the Grand Socco, slithering around peddlers stocking vegetables, hawkers waving and singing their wares, past the smell of roasting meat and smoke curling from sizzling coals, past Berber men in bright pantaloons—orange, red, striped—a cacophony of colors in the churning sun.

Across the square, Suzannah sat at a table in an outdoor café near the entrance to the Petit Socco. She raised her coffee cup and tilted her chin in the direction of the Grand Socco.

"Isn't that Tariq?" Lily asked.

"Where?" Drury whispered from between his teeth, scarcely moving his lips.

"Over there, in the Grand Socco."

"Don't gape at him," Drury muttered.

"What's he doing here?"

"Comes into town from time to time to sell chickens and fish. Has a permit to fish on Cape Spartel."

He passed through the Grand Socco without a blink in Tariq's direction. When Lily raised her arm to wave at Tariq, Drury pulled her along and kept them moving.

"Hurry," he said.

Lily stumbled after him. "Where are we going?"

Drury darted past women squatting in the sun next to their wares; past men hawking plates, bowls, meat, and leather from donkey carts.

He scuttled through the Street of the Silversmiths and into the Petit Socco, Lily at his heels.

The German followed.

They twisted through crowded streets, traversing alleys with blind walls, skirting hordes of children in school outfits.

"What's going on?" Lily asked, panting.

Faster, he pushed past crowded stalls and shops, past Berber women selling goat cheese and brooms and onions. They scrambled up and down steps through the congested streets. And still the German followed.

A warning to get out of the way, a cry of *"Balek, balek,"* came from behind. Lily turned to see a donkey laden with firewood trudging along the cramped alley. The German flattened himself against a doorway to let the donkey pass. Drury pulled Lily ahead of the donkey, turned one corner, then another.

Lily glanced over her shoulder. They had lost the German.

Drury threaded his way through a maze of narrow streets and paused before an ornate carved door set into a blue tiled arch covered with Kufic script.

"A mosque?" Lily asked.

"A medersa, a religious academy." Drury knocked on the door. "The mosque is next door."

A young man in a white djelaba opened a small entry cut into the door. Lily peeked into a serene, mosaic-tiled courtyard. In the center, a three-tiered fountain sparkled with water spilling from level to level.

Drury nodded to the youth at the door.

The boy nodded back. "He's expecting you. I'll fetch him."

The young man disappeared through the courtyard into a room hidden behind a colonnaded gallery.

"We're waiting for someone?" Lily asked.

"The Imam in charge of the medersa."

In a few moments, a lean man floated across the courtyard, a silk burnoose billowing behind him. He was thin and elegant with a handsome razor of a face adorned with a pointed goatee.

"*Sabach el kir,*" Drury said. "Good morning."

"*Sabach el nur.*" The man eyed Lily. "You bring a friend?" His nose halved his face like the beak of a bird.

"My assistant." Drury turned to Lily.

The holy man hesitated. "Welcome." He moved out into the alley and closed the door behind him and turned to Drury. "You bring a Romany woman here? To the house of Allah?"

"Lalla Sampson helps me to help you," Drury said.

Lily gave the Imam a tentative smile and stepped away from the door in deference to the holiness of the place.

The Imam made a circle with his thumb and forefinger and splayed out the other fingers of his right hand. "You see this?" he said, holding his hand against the calligraphy on the tiles around the doorway. "This is the name of Allah." The configuration of his fingers matched the writing behind them.

Lily looked from Drury to the Imam. She stepped further back.

Drury reached for her arm and guided her forward. "In the work we have to do, Lalla Sampson is needed."

"Nevertheless. A Christian woman in the medersa?"

Needed for what kind of work? Lily wondered.

"You must understand," the Imam said to Lily, tracing a graceful arc with his arm, his fingers still patterned in the name of Allah, "that when the French arrived, they brought bold women and new customs with them. The French were powerful and new, we were weak and old. We have yet to recover from the shock."

"Soon that will be over," Drury said.

"*Inshallah*. If Allah is willing. We must keep the same traditions. The same way to prepare food, the same way to make tea, the same way with the wind." His arms fell; his head bent to the side. "Still, slowly, slowly, we change. Wisdom comes from God. But haste comes from Satan." His voice trailed off.

"About the fifty thousand francs…" Drury said after a pause.

The holy man scanned the alley. "We cannot talk here. Someone will hear." He lowered his voice. "Tomorrow they will know, in Asilah, in Casablanca, as far away as Meknes. Rumors spread through the souk like lizards slithering across the pavement, through the stalls, from the spice sellers to the leather workers, from the wood carvers to the brass makers."

"Then meet us on The Mountain," Drury told him. "Tomorrow night."

The Imam nodded and smiled. He opened the door and turned to leave.

"In Marrakech, where I lived as a boy," he said over his shoulder, "going to the mountain meant starting a revolution."

"Right," Drury said. "Come to The Mountain and we'll drive out the French and Spanish."

In spite of her wariness, Lily felt a brief tremor of excitement.

"*Inshallah,*" the Imam said. "May it come to pass with the will of Allah."

He stepped over the threshold, back into the medersa, and closed the door behind him.

"What was that about?" Lily asked.

"He's a friend of the ghazi of the Moroccan Nationalist Party. They want economic and political opportunity, education."

"Doesn't everyone?"

"We can promote it, stir things up a bit. We call the Imam the Mekraj."

"Why? What does it mean?"

Drury didn't answer.

Chapter Nine

Drury appeared in the doorway with a tall man wearing an officer's uniform.

"Major Adam Pardo," Drury said. "Lily Sampson."

The major extended his hand. "Adam." When he leaned forward, the papers Lily had stacked on the edge of the desk fell to the floor.

The major looked up at Lily, his eyes as blue and brilliant as mosaic tiles. He knelt to pick up the papers. "So sorry." His face broke into a dazzling, apologetic smile. Lily caught her breath. He has a lot of teeth, she thought.

"Adam's G2," Drury said. "Army Intelligence."

Lily stood up to lean over the desk and watch him gather the fallen papers. "He seems brighter than that."

The major picked up the papers one by one and made a stab at putting them in some sort of order, then glanced up at her with another smile.

"Who's your dentist?" she asked.

"At the moment, just some guy in Gibraltar. But in real life, I go to a Dr. Steiner in Boston."

Armand Korian's sticky-sweet pipe tobacco wafted toward them from the corridor. He knocked on the open door and belched smoke into the room.

"Telephone." He aimed the stem of his pipe at Drury. "For you." He turned to leave. "In Boyle's office."

Drury gave Korian a grudging nod. "Be right back," he said and followed Korian down the hall.

The major continued to collect papers from the floor. "Drury tells me you can be trusted." He rose and stacked the papers on the side of Lily's desk.

"With what?"

"He tells me you're reliable, responsible, adaptable."

"That's right. Infallible, sensational, spectacular." Why would Drury discuss her character with a stranger?

"All that." He flashed his teeth again. "And more."

He leaned toward her, both hands on her desk. Lily flushed and backed away.

Korian passed the door and lingered a moment, openly curious. He gaped at them and moved on slowly, still peering into the office. The major tugged at his belt. His face had gone red. He looked down, brushed his sleeve with his hand.

Drury rushed down the hall to the office, pushed Korian out of the way and burst into the cubbyhole, white-faced. "Got to go."

"What happened?" Lily asked.

She watched Korian pause as he left, straining, poised to listen through the back of his head. She signaled Drury to wait.

Korian drifted down the hall, hesitating, moving on again, wavering, sauntering slowly back to his office.

"They arrested Suzannah," Drury said when Korian was finally out of sight.

The major looked startled.

"Got to go," Drury repeated.

"I'll go with you," the major said.

They scooted out, leaving the door open, and leaving Lily to wonder, in their wake, why Drury and Major Pardo were so concerned about Suzannah.

She shrugged, put the stack of papers in order, and went back to work and began to polish the final draft of a chapter on the politics of social change.

From time to time, Korian passed in the hallway, glancing in her direction. *He's waiting for me to start a conversation,*

Lily thought, find out what I'm working on. He wants to know everything. Just ignore him; just keep working.

In the early afternoon, Korian stopped in the doorway and leaned against the jamb, droopy-eyed, clearing his throat, running his finger along the bowl of his pipe, waiting for her to stop writing. Finally Lily looked up. He came into the room and leaned over the desk and stuck the pipe into his pocket.

"I was wondering, Lil…."

"My name is Lily."

"Sorry."

Korian leaned over her. His skin was pearly and yellowish, his eyes, lids dropping, held a peculiar glint.

"Are you all right?" she asked.

"Just tired."

She could feel his breath on her shoulder as she continued to edit the report. Korian lifted the pen from her fingers and put his hand over the foolscap pad. "I was wondering, Lily, if we could have dinner tonight. I know a place in the medina."

"I have to wash my hair."

"You have to eat too."

"Besides," she said. "You look like you need some rest."

Drury's voice came from the hall. "She's already made arrangements for dinner."

Korian looked up, his hand still on the report. "With you?"

Drury came into the room and walked over to the desk. "You're not the only pickle in the barrel." He lifted Korian's hand from the pad of paper and jostled him out of the way.

Korian's face flushed purple.

Drury lifted his chin as if standing his ground. "You look angry enough to spit." He held the pad in one hand, lifted a pencil from the tray on the desk and drummed on the table. "We have work to do. And so do you."

He waited.

Korian turned to go and Drury slapped the pad on Lily's desk.

"What happened with Suzannah?" Lily asked after Korian's footsteps faded down the hall.

"All taken care of." Drury sat down and tilted back in his chair. "False alarm. Some papal delegation is visiting. Guardia Civil picked up all the prostitutes. Imagine! Arresting prostitutes in Tangier." He smiled, snapped the chair upright and stood up.

He reached over to Lily's desk and began sorting pages, making corrections, collating them with ones he brought from his own batch of papers.

Lily cleared her throat. "Major Pardo…" she ventured.

"What about him?" Drury looked up. "He asked to meet you."

"Why? What does he want from me? You know him well?"

"We crossed paths when I was in graduate school. Came into the anthropology program in Columbia after I came back from my fieldwork."

"So it's *Doctor* Pardo?"

"He teaches at Harvard." Drury went back to the manuscript, correcting lines here, adding words there.

"What does Doctor Pardo want?"

Drury kept busy with the papers. "This is pretty good, as far as it goes." He tapped his fingers against the page he had been reading. "We ought to do a section on Concepts of the Supernatural. People love that."

"You mean the five pillars of Islam, that sort of thing?"

"Djinns, of course," Drury said.

"Like the 'Office of the Djinn'?"

Lily remembered.

Drury had haggled with a djinn in his "office" at the back of the cave during the excavation. Tariq and his brother Hasan had been muttering about djinns since Drury found the Neanderthal jaw.

Everyone knew, Hasan had warned them, that the djinn lived in old bones and relics. Each time they found a fragment of bone, Hasan would jump away, crying out, "*Ben Adam*? Is it human?"

Hasan always carried a bag of salt at his belt because, he told Lily, it was well known that djinns abhorred salt. Before he entered the cave each day, Hasan would sprinkle it on the ground, rub it on his clothes, and making a face, would swallow some, washing it down with great gulps of water.

Once Tariq took Drury aside and explained soberly, "Hasan thinks that the bones are here because this is the bureau of the djinn."

"Not to worry," Drury had told him. "I'll speak to the djinn."

Nothing happened until the day of the djinn, the day after Zaid had injured his eye, the day Zaid—hand on his forehead, a patch over his swollen eye—had remained in the villa in Tangier, lounging on the settee in a room off the garden.

Remembering what had happened to Zaid, Hasan had refused to enter the cave, lingering on the apron outside. Zaid was injured, Hasan insisted, because the djinn was angry that they had stolen his cache of bones.

After much argument and waving of arms, Tariq convinced his brother to get back to work. "You go outside," he told Hasan. "Work at the screen." The djinn would not venture into the light of the sun, Tariq assured him.

For most of the day, Tariq, with an air of resigned bravado, dug by himself in the trench. He hoisted the baskets of loose dirt to his shoulder with a groan, staggered out to Hasan, and dumped them into the rocker screen for his brother to sift.

Lily and Drury were working in the soft brown soil near an alcove in the back of the cave when they heard a cry from Tariq. "Ayeee! Ayee! *Bismillah rahman rahim*. In the name of God the merciful and compassionate."

Lily and Drury rushed to Tariq and found him sprawled across the trench, one leg sunken through the floor of the cave.

"He's fallen through." MacAlistair began tugging at Tariq's arm.

"It's the djinn," Tariq cried, thrashing and twisting, "pulling me down to the center of the earth."

"Stop caterwauling and climb out of there," Drury said and grabbed Tariq's other arm.

Together, MacAlistair and Drury yanked at Tariq, wrenching him this way and that while he bellowed and clamored for the mercy of Allah.

With one final jerk, they hauled Tariq clear of the trench.

Drury peered down through a funnel-like hole that opened to a glimpse of wild surf eddying against the rocks below. "He's broken through to the Lower Cave."

They released Tariq and he fell forward. His right arm shot out, clutching at MacAlistair's belt for balance. The other gripped MacAlistair's pants leg, near the pocket.

MacAlistair's keys spilled out. He reached for them, clutching air and lost his footing. Dazed, he watched the keys disappear into the foaming sea.

"Now how do we get home?"

"It was the djinn," Hasan whined, "the djinn."

"I'll deal with that irritating creature right now," Drury said.

He brushed his hand through his hair and stalked to the alcove in the back of the cave.

"Ayee!" Hasan whimpered. "He goes to the Bureau of the Djinn."

They heard Drury's voice roll and echo in the alcove. He argued and bargained in high-pitched Moghrebhi Arabic, answered in his normal tone in English and French, and searched through his pockets twice. Tariq watched from the cave entrance.

When he finished, Drury returned from the back of the cave. "Everything's fine. Convinced him to move the bureau to another cave. Snatched some hair from his head." Drury waggled a few strands of hair before Hasan's stupefied face. "Paid him for his trouble, of course."

"How much did you pay?" MacAlistair asked.

"Twenty centimes and a chocolate mint."

"And some kif," Tariq added.

"Is danger," Hasan told him.

"Nothing to worry about."

"Ayee. You must say prayers every day. Must fast on Ramadan. Must never drink alcohol, must never be unfaithful to your wife, never lie, never steal."

"I don't steal," Drury said. "And my wife doesn't give a damn." He waved the hair in the air and shoved it into his pocket. "If he bothers us again, I'll burn his hair and order him to leave."

"Bismillah rahman rahim," Tariq said.

Drury checked his watch. "Four o'clock," he said. "Time to go."

"How will we start the car?" MacAlistair asked.

But Drury had already left the cave and strolled down to the car.

He had crawled under the dash, hot-wired the Hillman, and then drove them back to town.

"Better not mention the Office of the Djinn," Drury was saying, looking over Lily's shoulder in the cramped space behind her desk. She crossed out the sentence she had just written.

"Remember, the Prophet himself preached to the djinn. Even converted some to the faith." Drury picked up the pages she had just finished.

Lily wondered if he could make sense of the ink splotches, arrows and additions in the margins, and the splattering of crossed-out words. "The pages look like they were wounded in the war. I'm not a great typist."

"Doesn't matter." He reached for the pile on the side of the desk, leafed through the pages, straightened the stack and arranged it neatly on the desk. "They can retype it."

At five o'clock, they left the Legation together. Outside the medina, they skirted the Grand Socco and approached a side street where Zaid waited in the Hillman, waited to drive up The Mountain to the villa, just as he did every evening.

Chapter Ten

MacAlistair sat at the piano in the salon, his fingers striking the keys, filling the room with furious music, arpeggio after arpeggio fleeing from his hand like frightened doves.

Under the colonnaded archway, Zaid leaned against the carved doors that opened on the courtyard. He had bleached his hair that week and a bright blond curl on his forehead stood out against his swarthy skin.

In the cool autumn dusk, under the open sky, a table had been laid for dinner next to the blue-tiled fountain. Idly, Zaid watched the servant, Faridah, dismantle the table setting, stacking bright earthenware plates into rickety piles, yanking off the white linen tablecloth. Tassels, fringing the scarf that covered Faridah's head, wavered disapprovingly in the evening breeze.

"Getting too cool to eat outside," Zaid said and pushed back his strand of yellow hair.

Faridah carried the dishes and cloth into the house toward the dining room. Strident piano chords reverberated against the tiles and quivered in the alcoves. The vibration made the copper lamps weave back and forth on their chains; lacy patterns of light on the walls swayed in dizzying arcs.

The effort made MacAlistair cough and he stopped playing. Sweat dripped from his temples; two flaming crimson patches on his cheeks stood out against the pasty whiteness of his face.

Zaid reached into his pocket for a cigarette. Drury watched Zaid with a bemused smile and dropped into a cushioned chair in the garden, looking away at the rose bushes, studying the mosaic pattern of the pavement.

"What are they angry about?" Lily asked Drury.

"Who?"

"MacAlistair and Faridah."

"Are they? I didn't notice."

A clatter of pots and dishes erupted from the kitchen. The odor of spices and cooking meat drifted out to them, mingling with the sweet perfume of roses, gardenias, and lemon trees in the garden.

"Faridah is making *pastilla* tonight," Zaid said.

"What's the matter with her?" Lily asked.

"It's nothing," Zaid said. "She's angry that her husband sends her out to work, doesn't let her keep the money."

"I didn't know she was married," Lily said.

Drury looked puzzled. He rose, scrutinizing Zaid with narrowed eyes. "Neither did I."

"Well, then," Lily said, "why the…."

"Come to the table," MacAlistair called from inside. "Faridah wants to leave early."

In spite of the tension in the house, Lily still savored the sensuous details of the room, the polished softness of the cushions, the intricately carved plaster of the walls and ceiling, the silken carpet, the corner vitrine made of burled thuza wood and filled with artifacts—Roman figurines, ancient pottery, bronze oil lamps, gold earrings the peculiar matte yellow of ancient gold.

She remembered the first time she had seen the cabinet.

MacAlistair stood next to her then. "My little collection," he said. "You see this." He opened the cabinet door and took out a decorated glass bead with a bearded, bug-eyed face. "The Phoenicians used these as charms to allay danger as they sailed past the Straits into the Atlantic. They stopped here in Tangier, ancient Tingis, to make sacrifices. According to legend, Tingis was founded by the son of Poseidon. Ancient Berbers lived here, Phoenicians, Carthaginians, Romans, long before Arabs and Europeans came."

He put the charm back. "And here," he reached into the cabinet and took out a marble bust mounted on a plinth of polished wood, "is the bust of a Berber youth from Volubilis." He looked over at Zaid and smiled, then lovingly ran his fingers along the tangle of curls on the head of the marble youth. "You must go to Volubilis, must dig there someday. It holds the heart of Morocco. The first Sultanate under Moulay Idriss began there. Latinized, Christian Berbers ruled there before the Moslems came. Romans ruled from there, Berbers, Phoenicians, Carthaginians ruled from there. And before that, Neolithic farmers lived there."

Faridah had dumped the forks on top of a stack of paper napkins in the middle of the table, and now she emerged from the kitchen with a tray of silver finger bowls and towels, her eyes steamy with resentment, sweat glistening on her upper lip. The tassels on her scarf bobbed as she plopped the finger bowls and towels in front of the diners and flounced back to the kitchen.

Drury waited until Faridah had left the room. "Tariq came into town today."

MacAlistair nodded in the direction of the kitchen. "Later," he said.

Zaid, watching silently, dipped his fingers in the bowl and dried them on the towel.

"By the way," MacAlistair said to Lily. "You're invited to tea tomorrow. At my aunt's—Emily Keane Shereefa of Ouzzane."

Her Highness, Emily Keane Shereefa, the duenna of British-Tangier society, was a legend, famous for her charities and good works.

Lily was impressed.

"She's your aunt?" Lily had seen her once, at a tea of the British Women's Association in the El Minzah. A small, frail woman in rustling taffeta, she had moved slowly and carefully through the reception area, leaning on the arm of her grandson Phillipe.

"My great-aunt. My grandmother was her sister. My mother brought me to see her when I was a child. She was beautiful and had a special way with children. I couldn't forget her. I fell in love with Morocco then—with everything Moroccan." He looked over at Zaid and smiled. "I returned for a visit after my mother died, and I've been coming back ever since."

Lily had heard that after Emily Keane's arrival in Morocco in the nineteenth century as governess for the children of the British consul, she had married Moulay Abdulsalam es Shereef, descendant of the Prophet, nephew of the Sultan, leader of the religious brotherhood of Ouzzane.

"She must be very old," Lily said. "Your aunt, I mean."

"Almost ninety."

Faridah cleared away the finger bowls and returned with a tureen of lentil soup. She plunked the tureen in front of MacAl-istair and stomped back to the kitchen.

"Quite an honor to be invited to tea with Emily Shereefa," Drury said, while MacAlistair ladled the soup.

"Will you be there?" Lily asked.

"Not tomorrow." Drury took a spoonful of soup. He turned to MacAlistair. "Tariq said he saw German U-boats near Cape Spartel."

MacAlistair put down his spoon and wiped his face with the napkin. "Inside the Straits? On the Mediterranean side?"

"He said they were…" Drury began. His voice trailed off as Faridah came into the dining room carrying a steaming dish almost as large as the table.

Drury waved his hand toward her in a gesture of approval and made a show of breathing in the aroma of the pastilla. "Magnifi-cent," he said to Faridah.

She paraded out. They waited until the clatter of pots came from the kitchen before anyone spoke.

"You can talk in front of her," Zaid said.

"No," MacAlistair said. "We can't." He dished the layers of filo dough, stuffed with pigeon and almonds, olives and sweet fruits, onto plates and passed them around.

"What happened today?" Drury asked.

"It's nothing," Zaid said. "She was looking at a book."

"What book?"

"Just a popular British novel," Zaid said. "One of those love stories women like."

MacAlistair picked up his napkin and threw it down again. "*Rebecca*. She found it at the bottom of a drawer in my wardrobe."

Drury frowned. "She reads English?"

Zaid leaned forward. "She doesn't read at all. She stole nothing."

The argument had a hidden significance that Lily couldn't fathom. She looked away and noticed movement behind the lattice that lined the shaded gallery of the upper floor. Drury followed her gaze as she watched the shadow pass from room to room.

"Get rid of Faridah," Drury said to MacAlistair. "Tonight."

MacAlistair sighed. "Go tell her she's fired," he said to Zaid.

Zaid scowled. "Who's going to wash the dishes?"

MacAlistair sighed again and held out his hands in entreaty.

Zaid stood up, slammed down his napkin, and strode out toward the kitchen.

"How long have you known him?" Lily asked after he was gone.

MacAlistair's face took on a dreamy expression. "I met him the first time I came to Morocco, a long time ago. He was working at the British Legation." His eyes seemed to smile at some secret memory. "He was so beautiful then. So graceful. When he danced, he seemed to float on a cloud, his feet just glancing the floor, his arms and hands tapering and elegant, moving like the wings of a magnificent butterfly."

MacAlistair paused, absorbed in memory, his eyes closed, his head swaying gently to the rhythm of a half-remembered tune.

"And he's been with you ever since?" Lily asked.

"We quarreled once, some silly thing, I can't remember now. He went to stay with his mother's family in Meknes, just south of Volubilis."

The shadow of a frown crossed MacAlistair's face. "He came back a year later, brought Faridah with him. He had changed, but I took him back, hired Faridah." He shrugged and gave Lily an apologetic smile. "He was still beautiful."

They could hear snatches of Faridah and Zaid talking in the kitchen, Zaid's voice a low hum, Faridah's raised a little, as if she were asking questions, then gushing out in a long spate, interrupted now and then by a grunt from Zaid.

Lily couldn't make out their words.

MacAlistair looked down at his plate, shaking his head regretfully. An embarrassed silence hung in the room.

"Tell me more about your aunt," Lily said into the silence. "It couldn't have been easy for her and the Sultan's nephew. Was their marriage accepted?"

"No. Her marriage to the prince scandalized both British and Moslem society. To make matters worse, she shocked the Moslem world by appearing in public, taking baskets to the poor, visiting the sick. The prince's reputation was destroyed and she discovered that children were dying of smallpox."

"That's when she began to work on getting them vaccinated?"

MacAlistair nodded and spread his hands on the tablecloth as if he were playing a chord on the piano. "She enlisted the help of the European community and moved to Tangier, hoping to save the reputation of her beloved prince. He died of grief two years after she left Ouzzane. She went on to wipe out smallpox in Morocco. Today, the Moslems regard her as a saint, and the Tangenos think of their marriage as a tragic love story."

Zaid came back into the room and sat down. "You tell her," he said to MacAlistair. "I can't."

"After she washes the dishes," MacAlistair said.

Faridah cleared the pastilla and brought tea. MacAlistair followed her into the kitchen. Soon the clatter of pots was drowned by Faridah's guttural shouts. After a few minutes, MacAlistair returned. They stayed at the table, sipping sweet tea in the cool night air until they heard Faridah leave.

MacAlistair glanced at his watch. "Time for us to look at the stars," he said to Drury.

Drury and MacAlistair rose from the table and left the room. Zaid took the cups to the sideboard and retrieved a deck of cards, a pad, and a pencil from the drawer. He slapped a package of Gauloises and a glass ashtray on the corner of the table and sat down to deal out cards to Lily and himself.

Scraping sounds of moving chairs came from the roof. The low murmur of voices, mingled with crackling and rasping noises, hovered above their heads.

Zaid fingered the cards, rearranged them, put one on the pile and reached for another.

"What's wrong with Faridah looking at a book?" Lily asked.

"That was just an excuse. Her brother died and I was comforting her. MacAlistair saw us in the garden with my arm around her. He was jealous." Zaid's lips curled around his cigarette, his eyes narrowed against the smoke. "It's the asthma, you know. Makes him irritable and suspicious of everyone. Sometimes he's difficult to live with."

Twittering and squawking noises from the roof filtered down to them.

"They have a short-wave radio up there, don't they?" Lily said.

Zaid puffed earnestly on his cigarette, picked up a card, breathed out a cloud of smoke, and spread his cards on the table.

"Gin."

Chapter Eleven

Herr Balloon waited outside, hiding below the steps behind the railing, when Lily left the Legation to go to tea at Lalla Emily's. This time she was ready for him.

She maneuvered past the vegetable stalls, up the hill in the crowded street, ducked into narrow lanes swarming with mothers and children, bustling with businessmen carrying briefcases and wearing dark djelabas. She reached the seedy confines of the Petit Socco, where gossips lounged in the Spanish cafés, exchanging rumors and sipping aperitifs. All the while, Herr Balloon stayed an interval behind her.

She wove through crowded streets to the Grand Socco, side-stepping storytellers and snake charmers, drugged monkeys and lion cubs, stalls that sold lizard's feet to cure diseases.

Once, she looked back. She thought she saw Korian and the German standing together. Just a glance exchanged between them, just a glance for a split second, and then Korian disappeared into the throng of milling people.

How could they know each other, she wondered. Maybe it's just my imagination.

The German hurried to catch up with her, and Lily took off again, plunging into the crowd.

She rushed ahead, until she heard the call, "*Balek, balek,*" from behind. It was what she had been waiting for.

She looked back to see a wood-seller leading a donkey overloaded with panniers of firewood. The creature plodded unsteadily among the stalls, the wood shifting from side to side as the ass stumbled through the crowd.

This time, as she knew he would, Herr Balloon did not stop. Lily halted. As Herr Balloon passed alongside the donkey, she ducked behind him, brought her knee up sharply into the back of his leg, and pushed him forward.

He careened into the donkey with a loud cry and fell to the pavement. A profusion of stacked wood cascaded over him. Lily ran, peered over her shoulder once to see a throng gathered around the wood-seller and Herr Balloon, and kept on running.

She hurried on through the crowded streets to tea.

"Moroccan houses," Lalla Emily was saying in a voice as thin as paper, "like hearts, look inward."

She wore a silk caftan richly embroidered with gold thread. Lily gazed at the elaborate mosaic pattern of the tiles on the wall and floor, the ponderous Venetian mirror, the carved balustrade that ran around the upper floor. Like so much else in the house, the tea was a blend of Moroccan and British traditions.

Lily, surprised to see Adam Pardo, wondered why he was here. The guests—Lily, MacAlistair, and Adam Pardo—sat on a divan that ran the length of the room. At a small table inlaid with mother of pearl, Lalla Emily poured tea into glasses crammed with mint leaves. Her thin hands, laced with veins, shook from the weight of the teapot. Her grandson Phillipe passed the glasses and a platter of pastry, heavy with honey.

The faint sound of the surf from the nearby beach reached them.

"I met my prince charming out there, on the strand," Lalla Emily said, waving in the direction of the water. "I had come to Morocco as a governess. We would ride along the sand every day, the children and I, to take the fresh sea air." She paused, the glass of tea in her hand, her eyes focused on some distant memory. "The first time I saw him, I fell madly in love."

"As did your prince," Phillipe said.

Lalla Emily put down the glass. "A sad day for both of us."

"Not so," MacAlistair said. "A great day for the children of Morocco."

She folded her hands in her lap. "My beloved Abdulsalam was the leader of the religious brotherhood of Tabiya in Ouzzane."

"Devout pilgrims flocked to Ouzzane to receive his blessing," Phillipe added.

Lalla Emily smiled at her grandson and stroked his hand. "I was a parson's daughter." She sighed and leaned back. "Like the good wife of an English clergyman, I took baskets to the poor, visited the sick." She looked down at her hands, shaking her head. "I was new to Morocco and naïve."

Upper-class Moslem women rarely ventured out in public —not to the markets where they sent their servants to shop, and certainly not to the houses of strangers.

"People in town must have been shocked," Lily said.

Lalla Emily nodded. "Appalled. But when I saw children and young mothers dying needlessly of diseases that could be prevented...." Her voice, already faint, quavered. "There was a smallpox epidemic, no vaccinations. They called the deaths the will of Allah. I raged against them, chastised them for believing in a cruel God."

Lily could imagine the scandal among the powerful Tabiya Brotherhood at the behavior of the wife of their hereditary leader. Since it had been established in the eighteenth century by a descendent of the Idrisides—the founding dynasty of Morocco—the brotherhood controlled the north and the district surrounding the remote hilltop town of Ouzzane.

Lalla Emily's eyes clouded over. "I couldn't stop. I was determined to inoculate the children of Morocco. I enlisted the help of the leaders of the European community, invited them to the house. The brotherhood was up in arms. I was consorting with nonbelievers in the house of their leader." She looked down at her hands again, her fingers twisting. "My husband was ruined, and I had ruined him."

She gazed at Lily as if seeking exoneration. "I had a cruel choice--between the lives of thousands of children and my love." She paused again. "I left Ouzzane and came here to Tangier to finish my work." Her hand brushed against her cheek. "My beloved died two years later. They tell me it was of a broken heart." She put her hand on Lily's arm. "Some day, you too may…."

Her voice trailed off with a sigh.

The room was hushed. Lily waited through the silence that hung in the air as grave as mourning.

Lalla Emily reached into her sleeve for a handkerchief and dabbed at the moisture that brimmed in her eyes. She turned to her grandson. "Phillipe, my dear, will you play for us?"

Phillipe put down his glass and went to a piano in the adjacent room. Lily reached for her glass of tea, then set it back down and listened as the strains of a Chopin nocturne, liquid and eloquent, washed over them.

"Our family always has shown musical talent," said Lalla Emily, her head bent, intent on the sound. "If you will excuse me, I leave you to your business."

She rose, lifting herself with the help of a gold-headed cane with an intricate chased pattern. Leaning heavily on the smooth, well-worn handle, she moved slowly into the courtyard and closed the door behind her.

MacAlistair and Pardo looked at each other, then at Lily. She tried another sip of the hot tea.

"First of all," Pardo said. "What we talk about here must never leave this room."

"Why so mysterious?" Lily tried the tea again. It burned her throat.

"You've heard of the OSS?" Pardo asked Lily.

"It's a branch of G-2?"

"Office of Strategic Services. Civilians. Technically, it's under G-3, Organization and Training Division."

"Why are you telling me this?"

"The OSS uses experts, specially trained personnel, university professors—linguists, archaeologists, anthropologists like Drury—for activities outside regular military channels."

So that's what Drury was up to. Lily had heard rumors about some kind of work by Ruth Benedict, Margaret Mead, and Rhoda Metraux—all former students of Franz Boas, who had founded the department of anthropology at Columbia.

Some of this made sense to Lily now. "You and Drury were Boas' students at Columbia, weren't you?" She paused and thought some more. "You're talking about the National Character Studies, Culture at a Distance projects? The kind of thing we're working on at the Legation?"

"That's for the Office of War Information, OWI. I'm talking about the OSS."

"It's all alphabet soup to me."

"Archaeologists like Nelson Glueck work for the OSS."

Lily knew that Nelson Glueck, director of the American School of Archaeological Research in Jerusalem, was conducting an archaeological survey of Transjordan. "So Glueck's not just doing a survey?" Lily asked. "He's mapping out terrain and military installations?"

Pardo nodded. "Right. The job of the OSS is to get ahead of the Army and Navy, lay the groundwork for them. Find out things. Make contacts they can't." He spoke slowly, carefully, as if he expected her to take notes. "The thing is, anthropologists, archaeologists can go anywhere. It's the nature of their work. Before you came, Drury checked you out. And we've done some background work on you. For security clearance."

"You want me to do a survey?" she asked.

"Not exactly. This is more urgent. You're on the ground here. OSS headquarters for North Africa is here in Tangier."

"Oh, for God's sake," MacAlistair said. "Get on with it." He leaned forward, his hand on his knee. "This spring and summer, our forces broke the German drive to Egypt. Rommel retreated back into Libya, ending the threat to Suez. Now it's time to attack Rommel from the west, destroy Axis forces in the Western Desert, push him out of Africa."

"We have to get a foothold in North Africa," Pardo said. "Secure bases for intensified military operations against the Axis in Europe. It takes a lot of personnel. We need help—people like you who know the Middle East—to prepare a local underground for backup."

MacAlistair stood up. "Drury has been working with the Riffians. They're ready to step in, if needed."

"We work through the Moroccan Nationalist Party," Drury had told her. *"They despise the French."*

"If Drury signals them," MacAlistair said, "they'll assemble and seize a few key positions, cut off roads, garrisons, deliver guns. The Americans will handle Morocco and Oran, land troops, drop parachutists. We'll be further east." He coughed gently and placed his hands on the small of his back, stretched, and coughed again and waited for the paroxysm to finish. "Our convoy's already left Glasgow and Liverpool. In a few days it will be poised off the coast of North Africa."

Lily wondered what her place in this was. "Well then, why—?"

"Here's the point." MacAlistair moved an armchair closer to the divan and sat down. "Tangier is going to be communications HQ here in North Africa for Operation Torch, relaying messages between Casablanca and Gibraltar."

Lily stared at the tea glass and curled her fingers around it. "Operation Torch?"

"That's the code name for the landings in North Africa," Pardo said. "I'll be in Casablanca. You'll assist Drury in Tangier. Think you can handle it?" He paused. "Think about it. If you agree, there's no turning back."

Chapter Twelve

Lily started back to the Legation. Bits of paper, scuffed shoes and slippers, scraped along the street in her peripheral vision. She needed to think, to ponder what she had just heard, to be by herself before she went up to The Mountain.

Her sandals flapped against the crooked sidewalk.

Assist Drury.

What would she have to do? How would she do it? What would her duties be?

She gave a perfunctory nod to the marine on duty, entered the Legation and started down the hall to her office. The building had the feel of afternoon drawing to an end: doors clicking shut, typewriters stilled, drawers closing.

She opened her office. Korian stood at the desk, rifling through the top drawer.

When she spoke, her voice was cold. "You'll find nothing of value there."

He looked up, eyes alert, fingers moving. "I was looking for a paper clip." He closed the drawer and shoved his hands in his pockets.

What was he really looking for?

"Ask the secretary."

"The secretary's already left for the day."

"So should you." Lily moved into the room.

"I'm working late." Korian had edged away from the desk and started out of the office.

"So I see."

"I didn't think you'd mind," he said from the door.

After this, Lily vowed, I'll always lock the desk.

The Mekraj was already at the villa, seated in the garden talking to Drury, when Lily arrived.

"We need a new mosque, for the grandeur of Allah," he was saying. "With a new minaret, proud as a finger, that shows Allah in his uniqueness."

"With a great golden door," Drury added.

"Not so. The door must be humble and small, to show that humans are humble and small. But inside must be large, like the glory of Allah. When you cross the line through the sacred door, you bow your head, you wash away the thoughts of the world and enter a different place."

"You shall have your mosque, you shall have your minaret, tall and square, reaching to the heavens, calling the faithful from every corner of the earth."

The Mekraj glanced at Lily and MacAlistair standing in the corner of the garden, then back to Drury.

"It's all right," Drury said. "They're working with us."

"Secrets, secrets," the Mekraj said. He turned to Lily and MacAlistair. "You cannot know a city until you enter its gates, you cannot know the Moroccan house until you set foot inside, you cannot know a woman until she removes her veil."

The Mekraj poured the tea, arcing the amber liquid with a flourish into mint-filled glasses on the tray in front of him.

"You see," he said, gesturing at the tea tray that sat on a mother of pearl inlaid table, "the entire universe is here. The sinia," he pointed to the polished copper tray, "is the earth, the teapot is the sky, and the glasses hold the rain that falls when it unites the earth with the sky."

He cradled the hot glass in his hand and sipped, then put it down. "Our warriors are brave."

"But now they must be like snakes," Drury told him. "Strike and hide, strike and hide."

"After the great Moulay Yousef conquered Marrakech," Imam Tashfin said, "he was inspired by Allah to carry his warriors across the Mediterranean, to bring Allah and make order on the Iberian continent. We can do no less for our own land."

"Then we can count on your help if need be?" asked MacAlistair.

"A good man keeps his word. When I get the forty thousand francs to help build the mosque, my followers will know we must establish order. They are brave, very brave warriors, the sons of warriors, and men of peace."

"Forty thousand francs?" Drury said. "Zaid told me fifty thousand."

"Ah," said Imam Tashfin. "Forty thousand for Allah and ten thousand for Zaid."

"Zaid is taking a cut? Zaid is trying to cheat me?"

"Zaid is not an evil man. Not yet. But his soul wanders. It is caught in the twilight between the world of the Romany—what you call the western world—and the world of Islam. He tries to cure his soul with greed. Some day he may slip on the greed and fall into the abyss."

MacAlistair had been sitting on the low wall that encircled the garden. Now he stood up. "Not Zaid. I know him…." His voice trailed off and he looked into the distance. "I know him well, for a long time, a very long time. He's earned my trust over and over."

The Mekraj looked at him and sighed. "Each man's destiny is different. They can be next to each other, wear the same dress, eat the same food, but their destiny is not the same."

"We may need your help very soon," Drury said.

Zaid appeared in the corner of the garden and Lily wondered if he had been listening. He sauntered toward them, his brow furrowed, his hands stiff against his sides.

"We were speaking of making a miracle," Drury said to Zaid.

The Mekraj held his glass between his thumb and index finger and sipped. "It says in the Koran that a miracle will come out of the West." He turned to Lily and smiled. "Morocco was always

Al Maghreb Al Aqsa, the farthest west, at the edge of the Sea of Darkness. Beyond that, there was nothing."

"But—" Lily said.

"Ah," the Mekraj said. "You are going to say that you come from beyond the Sea of Darkness."

Lily nodded.

"Our wise men tell us that the Prophet knew of the lands beyond the Sea. But in the days of the Prophet, Allah was not known there, it was nothing but a great void until men from Andaluse brought Allah to them. Then the lands blossomed and entered the world."

"A miracle will truly come out of the West." Drury leaned toward him. "From beyond the Pillars of Hercules, out of the Sea of Darkness. It will lead you back to the golden age, back to the days when you ruled Andalusia. But you must help."

"What miracle?"

"Within a week, it will rise out of the sea," Drury said. *"Bismillah*, in the name of Allah."

"May it come to pass. *Inshallah*. God willing." He lifted the hood of his djelaba. "And the fifty thousand francs for the new mosque?"

"In the bank tomorrow."

"Tell Tariq to come to the Friday mosque. Tell him to bring the fish that you catch in Andaluse." The Mekraj draped the hood of the djelaba over his fez, enveloping his face in shadow, and turned toward the door. *"Inshallah,"* he whispered. The word wafted after him and floated in the air like the flutter of the djelaba in his wake.

"Well, that's done," Drury said.

All this time, Zaid hadn't moved. He leaned against the pillar, his arms crossed across his chest and watched, thin-lipped and angry-eyed, from the corner of the garden.

"What does Mekraj mean?" Lily asked.

"The samovar we use to boil water for tea," Zaid said. "You know why they call him the Mekraj? Because they use him to stir things up and boil them over."

"Zaid—" MacAlistair began.

Zaid turned to face him. "You ridiculed him. You spoke to him as if he were a fool."

"He's provincial," Drury said. "He believes in miracles. Anyway, he's getting fifty thousand francs."

"And a little kif to dream on," added MacAlistair.

Zaid turned to MacAlistair. "You're just like the rest of them, aren't you?" His voice was husky with anger.

"I didn't mean anything by it."

The glimmer of tears poised on the rim of Zaid's eyes. "All these years I've trusted you. And you've been laughing behind my back with your cheerful British racism."

MacAlistair looked away.

"We have to go upstairs to send the news," Drury said. "Come on, let's go."

When their footsteps sounded on the stairs, Zaid started toward the dining room. The button of his sleeve caught in the carved Arabesques of the pillar. He yanked at it, tearing his cuff.

"Damn." He pulled off the button, frowning, and glanced at Lily. "You heard what they said. You Americans want to take over Morocco. You can't be trusted, any more than the British. You're no better than the French," he said. "No better than the Spaniards. You're all here to steal our land."

Chapter Thirteen

"This time, we leave the hotel a different way," Drury said.

They took the elevator down to the Wine Bar and went through a long hallway to a back door and almost tripped over a heap of clothing and tins piled by the steps.

"What's this?" Lily asked.

"The British Charitable Society," Drury told her. "Once a week they collect clothing and canned goods for the bountiful English ladies to distribute to the poor."

They left by a narrow alley, pushed their way through the crowds of the fondouk market, went down a stepped street, across a square, and through the white arch that led to the Legation.

"Much better," Drury said.

◇◇◇

Lily settled at the desk in the musty little office at the Legation while Drury went down the hall to see Boyle.

It was almost noon when Drury returned. "I've an appointment for lunch. Have to go. Back around two."

Before he left, he leaned over her shoulder to read a page of the pamphlet. "Looks pretty good," he said. "We'll be finished tomorrow."

"About Zaid." Lily hesitated a moment before she went on. "I don't think you can trust him."

"What makes you say that?"

"Well, there's Faridah, for one thing—"

"She's just a Berber from the Atlas Mountains. Forget about her."

"And Zaid resents colonialism."

"They all do. Wouldn't you?" Drury ran his finger along his upper lip, then nodded. "We can use that, you know. Promise him a free Morocco when all this is over."

"You think he'll believe you?"

"What choice does he have?"

Korian's footsteps sounded in the corridor. He paused, scowling when he saw Drury. Korian's left eye was swollen and discolored.

Drury eyed him with overt delight. "See you ran into a door."

"I'll get you for this." Korian's face flushed, and he choked with thin-lipped hatred. "You'll be sorry you ever met me. I'll get you for this." He stomped down the hall and clattered into the stairwell.

"If anyone's not to be trusted, it's him," Drury said in his wake.

Lily nodded. "You're probably right," she said and told Drury about seeing Korian with the German, and about finding him rummaging through her desk.

"A few other things about him," Drury said and sat down. "Did some checking about the effect of the propaganda in the Legation bulletin. According to Boyle, Korian is responsible for distribution. I asked Korian what he does. He said his staff makes a couple hundred copies, slips them under doors and in mailboxes during the night. I made inquiries among merchants and civil leaders, asked what they thought about the bulletin. No one in Tangier outside of the Legation ever heard of the bulletin." He slapped his hand on the desk. "Korian pocketed the money. Never distributed the bulletin."

"What are you going to do?"

"Already did it. Confronted Korian. He denied it, of course, said I just didn't understand the locals. So I punched him in the nose, knocked him down."

"You what? That's how he got the black eye?"

Drury grinned, clapped Lily on the shoulder, and swaggered out.

What's wrong with that man? Lily wondered, and shrugged. None of my business. Time to get back to work.

She sat at the desk and skimmed through the pages. The pamphlet was turning out better than she thought. She concentrated on the work, hunched over the desk, and didn't notice Adam Pardo until he knocked on the open door and smiled his remarkable smile. "Want to go for lunch?"

"Is it that late, Major Pardo?" Lily looked at her watch. She was beginning to get hungry. "I'll get a sweater. Where do you want to go?"

"I don't know Tangier that well, just arrived a few days ago."

Lily gave it some thought, remembered he was G2. "I know just the café for you, Major. It's in the Ville Nouvelle, the new city."

"My friends call me Adam." He leaned forward with a puzzled look. He reached for something on Drury's desk, glanced at it, and held it in his hand.

"What's that?" Lily asked.

"Some playing cards."

Lily looked at the cards he held in his hand with a familiar blue and white pattern of circles and leaves and swirls. "How did they get here?"

"They weren't here before?" he asked.

Had she been so engrossed in the pamphlet that she didn't notice someone come into the office? "Not that I remember."

They're only playing cards, she thought. Nothing sinister. They weren't even exceptional playing cards.

"When I was a child, we used to collect playing cards and trade them with each other. That's the commonest pattern, that and the red one like it. They weren't worth much. But some cards had beautiful scenes, paintings. They were worth more, sometimes as much as five or six of those in a trade."

"We collected baseball cards. They came in packs of bubble gum. We'd trade them, or flip them, match them against each other."

"Did you win?"

"Sometimes. Sometimes the cards got bent."

He turned over the cards in his hand and fanned them out. Lily saw his eyes widen with concern.

"What is it?"

"A dead man's hand."

"What's that?"

"A pair of eights and a pair of aces. It's the hand Wild Bill Hickok was holding when he was killed. Shot in the back in a saloon in Deadwood, South Dakota."

"Wild Bill?"

Adam clutched the cards closed and put them in his pocket. "Whoever left them here...."

Lily finished it for him. "Knows about American folklore and knows Drury's friend Donovan."

"I'll get word to Drury," Adam said, "soon as he comes back. Meanwhile, let's get some lunch."

They left the Legation and climbed the steps of the fondouk market, snaking past vendors and fruit sellers.

"You given any thought to what we talked about yesterday?" Pardo asked.

"Curing smallpox?"

"Anthropology. You come highly recommended."

"By whom?" Lily asked. "Recommended for what?"

"You do that very well." They had reached the Ville Nouvelle. "You know what I want to talk about."

They approached the Place de France, just a few blocks past the El Minzah. "Here it is," Lily said. "The Café de Paris." They settled at an outside table with a view of the bay. "I had to show you this. I think you'll be amused."

Most of the tables at the café were taken. Even the woman with the poodle was there. Germans, Italians, Frenchmen, leaning close, murmuring in low voices, eyes shifting from side to side, scanning the tables over their wineglasses, furtively eaves-dropping like the cast of a comic opera.

They twisted their way to an empty table near the door of the café.

"What is this place?" Pardo asked as they sat down. "A union hall for spies? They're all looking into the soup of the man at the next table."

"That's about it, Major. They all come here to make deals, pick up the odd rumor, sell it to whoever pays best."

"Adam. My name is Adam."

She inclined her head. "Adam."

A waiter approached and handed them a flyspecked menu, one side in French, the other in Arabic. Lily scanned the street. Herr Balloon came toward the square, crossing from El Minzah. The left side of his face was swollen and bruised. She watched while he took a seat at a nearby table. He hadn't noticed her yet.

"There's an epidemic of black eyes in Tangier," Lily said. "We'd better leave before we catch it. Let's get out of here."

"The idiot behind me is reading your menu." Pardo, on the verge of laughter, leaned back in his chair, enjoying himself too much to leave. "Look over there." He indicated a man hiding his mouth while he whispered, his face moving in time to sibilant noises coming from behind his hand. "Trying to act like he's just picking his teeth."

Lily smiled as the man's little finger scratched along the side of his lip. She noticed Herr Balloon watching her.

She put down the menu. "Let's go." She stood up.

Adam was still looking around, grinning. "What's the hurry?"

But she was already wedging her way through the tables.

Adam hurried to catch up. "Something bothering you?" he asked. "That German with the bruised face at the table over there?"

"You said you wanted to talk."

She started down the street toward the El Minzah. Adam followed. She glanced back at the Café de Paris to Herr Balloon and his cohort speaking to the waiter.

Beyond them, Lily caught sight of Suzannah strolling with an officer of the Guardia Civil, smiling, her arm linked in his. Suzannah's face seemed lit with adoration. She nodded as she spoke, her head inclined, her eyes intent on her companion, seeming to dote on every word the officer said.

Lily stopped. "Suzannah!"

"What about Suzannah?"

"Over there, with a Spanish officer."

"Where?"

But they had turned the corner by the time Adam looked back and Suzannah and her escort were already gone.

Herr Balloon still sat hunched over a table, his arms crossed in front of him, frowning at a menu.

"You know him?" Adam asked. "The German, I mean."

"Not to speak to. He's been following me."

"Drury mentioned him. The one who planted the microphone. He follow you yesterday to Lalla Emily's?"

"He tried. He didn't get far. That's how he got the bruises."

"You knocked him down?"

"He ran into a donkey."

"And you convinced the donkey to stand still so he could run into it," Adam said.

"Something like that."

"Drury told me you have hidden talents."

"I'm more concerned about Suzannah. What was she doing with the Spaniard?"

"Just plying her trade."

Adam strode ahead of her, clearing a path around the snake charmers and kebob chefs in the Grand Socco, passing the old cannons in the gardens of the Mendoubia.

"Doesn't it bother you that she's in contact with the Guardia Civil?" Lily asked when she caught up with him.

"What's to be bothered?"

They had reached the Bab el Kasbah and crossed over toward the beach.

"We can walk along the sand." Adam scanned the street behind them. "No one's followed us. We can talk there, no one will hear."

The bright autumn air was brisk and clear with the smell of the sea. A breeze came off the Mediterranean.

"No one will hear what?"

"I'm recruiting you."

"For what, exactly?"

"You'll be working with Drury, have to deal with local French authorities across the border, Free French, Colons, Arabs, Berbers."

A whiff of excitement, a flush of anticipation, stirred her.

"Colons?" she asked.

"French, Spanish, Italians, Colonials. Think you can do it?"

I have no idea, Lily thought.

"Of course I can," she answered.

Don't botch it.

"You'll operate secret radio networks, smuggle arms, build reliable connections with the natives."

I could do that. I could do that, she thought. Why else am I an archaeologist? Some people grow up and learn to live in quiet houses. Not me, she thought, not me. I can travel to mysterious places, live in lost times, and come away unscathed.

"This is the Near East," she said. "Will they trust a woman?"

"That's the point. You have the best cover. You look as innocent as a toy poodle."

She tried to hide her escaping smile. "You want me to play Mata Hari?"

"Not exactly."

He stopped, faced her, and watched as the wind whipped against her skirt and blew back her hair. "But I'll bet you'd be good at it."

"I've smuggled arms before."

"Don't tell me about it."

"Just accidental. I did field work in Palestine. I had a friend in the Hagannah. We came across an arms cache, and—"

Adam glanced at her. "You think that's news?"

"What else do you know about me?" she asked.

"As much as I need to."

"Don't I have to be interviewed?"

"You've already been interviewed."

"By Drury's friend Donovan?"

Adam nodded.

"It wasn't much of an interview."

"It was enough. He knows all about you."

"Drury told me that Donovan is very persuasive, that nobody can refuse him."

"That's about right."

Lily shrugged and spread out her fingers. "Who am I to break with tradition?"

◇◇◇

Lily and Adam sauntered toward the water's edge, each step heavy in the clean sand. Seagulls soared past them, folding and unfolding their wings.

"I don't want you to get hurt," Adam said. "I want you to succeed, not to take unnecessary chances. Not go for glory. Not like Drury." He paused and kicked at the sand. "This is a job that must be done. Drury is like a child. Somebody asks, 'You want to get yourself killed?' and he answers, 'Of course, of course.'" He turned to face Lily. "What's wrong with him? An unhappy marriage?"

"Maybe. He married the department secretary. The rumor was that after the wedding, his wife spent more time in the psychiatric ward of Cook County than she did at home. You know how gossip flies around in academia."

"She was a volunteer?"

"She was a patient."

"I heard the same, but I wasn't sure. It's hard to picture him as Brontë's Rochester. Any children?"

"That's another rumor. They say he has a mistress in Paris and had a child with her. It's possible. He went to Paris every year and stayed in France a while, no matter where he was doing field work."

"Maybe just to change planes." He gave a quizzical shrug. "Or buy some Brie at the airport."

"Sure. He'd stay for a month, sometimes two. That's a lot of Brie."

"You think he's a little crazy?"

"I don't know. He told me once that he had always wanted to climb strange mountains, stir up tribes, work secretly to destroy an enemy," Lily said.

She could understand that, dreaming of adventure in exotic places, enmeshed in mysterious intrigue, flirting with imaginary danger, emerging unharmed and triumphant.

"This is different. This is no swashbuckler's fantasy," Adam said. "This is real. And lives depend on it."

A small lizard, a sand racer, scudded past them, leaving its track along the damp sand.

"Lizards are talismans against evil," Lily said. "You think I should carry one with me? Pin it on my lapel, wear it on a chain?"

"You don't need talismans." Adam searched her face. "We'll make a good team."

A sudden gust came off the sea and billowed through Lily's skirt. She bent over and clasped it with her fingers, holding it down against the wind. "I'm getting chilly. Come on. I know a great restaurant with a terrific view."

She led them back to the Bab el Kasbah, up the steps, under arches and up another flight of stairs. They climbed uphill through the medina, through white streets, past houses hidden behind high, blank walls.

"Tell me," Lily said, "what else do you know about Drury? He's a bit of a racist, isn't he?"

Adam stopped and pursed his lips.

"I mean," Lily continued, "he has a theory that different races developed at different times, and some are more advanced than others. Cro-Magnons are the most highly evolved, according to him."

They had stopped walking now, and Adam shifted his foot. "What do you think of his theory?"

"I once told him that if he mapped the distribution of classic Neanderthals and that of blue-eyed blondes, they would probably overlap. I told him that blue eyes and blond hair are Neanderthal vestiges, that he and I were probably their descendants."

"You told him that?"

She nodded.

"What did he say?"

"He was upset. Told me I didn't know what I was talking about."

"Like a true Neanderthal." Adam flashed a smile at her and started up the hill. "Drury first came here by way of France in 1924, together with MacAlistair. He had romantic dreams of the Rif coast, the tall cliffs and hidden bays where smugglers and pirates of the Barbary Coast hole up. He was fascinated with stories he heard of the Rif—Nordic tribes in Africa, fighting for their independence."

"Is that how he met Abd el Krim?"

"Not that time. He didn't get to see the Rif. But he and MacAlistair formed a lasting friendship. Later, they came back to Morocco together, MacAlistair as a journalist, Drury as an anthropologist. Drury did his field work among the Rif."

They climbed past the goldsmith shops of the mellah, up and up toward the quiet of the Kasbah.

"And MacAlistair?" Lily asked.

"He's SIS, Secret Intelligence Service, the British equivalent of OSS. When he came here in the Twenties, he was intrigued by the exotic paintings of J.F. Lewis and Delacroix. He wrote pieces for the *London Times* about the exotic mystery of the Near East, how Delacroix captured the sweep of the garments, the dignity and elegance of the men, the beauty of the women, the architecture, the intricate geometric designs of the fascias and plaster arches. Brits eat up that stuff."

"What about Zaid?"

"Raised in Manchester, half-English, half-Moroccan. He had a rough time in England. At school, they treated him like an outsider. So he came back to Morocco. MacAlistair befriended him. And now, MacAlistair depends on him for everything. I don't think he could survive without him."

Lily thought of the conversation at the dinner table the other night. "There's a strong bond between MacAlistair and Zaid."

Adam glanced over at her and raised his eyebrows. "You don't really want to know about that."

"The love that has no name?"

"I believe the phrase is 'the love that dare not say its name'."

"And now Zaid does the contacts with the Berbers?" Lily said.

"What makes you say that?"

"Half a Rif is better than none."

"Half a Moroccan. We have other uses for Zaid."

"Such as?" But she already knew.

"Each person only knows about his or her own job. It's safer that way. One rank up knows the jobs of those under him and a little more. The only one who has the whole picture is Ike. Maybe Churchill and Roosevelt."

"So you're telling me that a Moroccan in the villa is worth two in the Atlas Mountains."

"I didn't say that."

"Do you trust Zaid?"

Adam paused, gave it some thought. "He worked for the SIS once, has full security clearance."

"He still has it?"

"Sometimes he champs at the bit, wants to know more than is good for him. He'd rather give orders than take them."

They paused at a belvedere perched on a pinnacle of the Kasbah, above the sea wall. They took in the view of the port and the white curve of the beach as far as Malabath.

"Over there, across the water," Adam said, pointing, "that gray mass in the mist, that's Gibraltar. You see that white speck against the haze? That's the ferry that goes back and forth across the Strait."

Swallows swooped and chattered, struggling against the wind, making wide arcs around the sea wall.

"Allied headquarters are there. The place is honeycombed with tunnels dug in the eighteenth century when the Brits were fighting off attacks from the French and Spanish to maintain control of Gib."

They began walking again, strolling leisurely across a white square behind the old fortress of the Kasbah.

"And you?" Lily asked. "What about you?"

"I did my field work in Canada, among the Ojibwa."

"I mean now. How long have you been stationed in Tangier?"

"Just got here, the day I met you. Before that, I was in the Western Desert."

Lily tensed and stopped walking. Rafi. "With the British Eighth Army?"

Adam nodded.

She turned to face him. "Were you at Tobruk?"

He shook his head. "Attached to them long after that. Wasn't with them 'til the second Battle of El Alemein."

Still, he might know something about Rafi. "You hear anything...." She leaned forward intently, as if her urgency could compel Rafi to be safe. "Anything," she repeated, "about who made it out, got away from the Germans?"

"Only a handful made it." Adam looked down at the pavement and shook his head. "Eighth Army was decimated when Tobruk fell. Rommel took three hundred thousand prisoners, all the supplies."

"Who was in the handful?"

"Less than four hundred men. Some Coldstream Guards and South Africans managed to break out of the perimeter in lorries. Made it as far as the Egyptian frontier." Adam thought a minute and smiled. "Some New Zealanders broke through to Rommel's headquarters, set it afire. Gave Rommel a scare. Those Anzacs are something else. During Rommel's attack on Alemein, they held the Quattara depression, turned him back."

Maybe Rafi went with the Anzacs, Lily thought. Maybe he went on to Cairo. Rafi can't get in touch with me because he doesn't know where I am. That's why I don't hear from him. I must find a way to let him know I'm in Tangier.

Adam's voice broke into her thoughts. "Nothing to worry about. Things are better since Montgomery took over. We've provided Sherman tanks. And better anti-tank missiles—4.2 armor-piercing mortars with delayed fuses. We'll do all right in Torch." Adam sniffed the air. "Weather's changing."

Lily started up a flight of stairs that led to a restaurant door.

Adam paused at the landing. "Whatever you decide, I have to warn you. If there's trouble, you're on your own." He pushed the door open and held it. "We're going inside?"

Lily hesitated a moment. She squared her shoulders, and with a nod, glided through the door.

"You want the tajine?" she asked and smiled. "I recommend it."

Chapter Fourteen

Bits of paper and flotsam flew before the morning wind, whipping around stalls of the Grand Socco. Berber women hovered over baskets of vegetables like flapping birds and held onto broad brims of hats that curled in the blustery weather.

"There's a Levanter blowing," Drury said. "Rainy season will start soon. It's getting late."

"Late for what?" Lily asked.

Drury hurried on ahead toward the Legation, while Lily scurried after him. "Late for what?" she asked again before she realized that he was worried about the weather for the landings of Torch.

He bustled back and forth all morning, from Lily's desk to his own, no time to talk, collating sections of the report, urging Lily to hurry the final corrections.

He left the office and Lily concentrated on finishing the report, hunched over the desk. Tired, she paused and closed her eyes.

Someone's hands began to knead her stiff shoulders. Drury?

It felt good. She rested and leaned back.

The sweet odor of Korian's pipe, mixed with overtones of garlic and sweat hit her nostrils. She jumped out of the chair.

"You're working too hard," Korian said, smooth and oily. "That's why you're so edgy."

He leaned over her desk to read what she had written.

She turned the paper over. "The report will be circulated to all personnel when it's ready."

The swelling around his eyes had softened, leaving only a slight greenish discoloration. His lapel had a hole, charred around the edges.

"You burned a hole in your suit."

"Must be from the pipe. I'll get it rewoven." He looked down and brushed at it with the side of his hand. "That's not why I wanted to see you. I thought we could have dinner tonight."

She moved away from the desk. "I'm busy."

"Have to wash your hair again?" He tried an unctuous smile. "All work and no play." He moved nearer and rested a hand on her shoulder.

She backed away. He edged closer. She could feel his breath on her face, panting, smelling of yesterday's garlic.

Drury appeared at the door. He cleared his throat, brandished a fist, and Korian threw up his arms in a gesture of surrender before he scurried out.

"Thanks," Lily said.

"He's a pea-brained idiot." Drury closed the door and reached into his pocket. "Time for you to earn your keep." He handed her a ticket. "Tomorrow you go to Gibraltar. You'll be leaving on the nine o'clock ferry."

"Did Adam talk to you about the Dead Man's Hand?"

"He told me. Nothing to worry about. Just some joker trying to frighten us." Drury began sorting the pages on Lily's desk. "There's a leak. I think I know who it is."

"You're not going to do anything about it?"

"Of course I am. I'm going to use it to our advantage."

Lily turned over the ticket in her hand, wondering what she was supposed to do in Gibraltar. "About Gibraltar…" She looked up to ask Drury. But he had already left and closed the door behind him.

He wouldn't have answered anyway.

◇ ◇ ◇

By four o'clock, Drury had gathered the remaining scattered pages of the report together, arranged them in sections with a paper clip, and typed out a table of contents.

"We're done," Drury said. "That's it."

He carried the draft into Boyle's office. Lily followed.

Drury flung the manuscript on Boyle's desk with a flourish. "Our pamphlet. A masterly work, if I say so myself. With this pamphlet in hand, victory is guaranteed."

Boyle put on his glasses, held the battered manuscript at arm's-length, and looked skeptical.

"Your office can do the final typing," Drury told him.

Boyle placed his glasses carefully on his desk and turned to Lily. "Thank you, Miss Sampson."

"About Korian—" Drury said.

"Glad you brought it up. What about Korian? I don't take kindly to fisticuffs against people on my staff."

"It's the bulletin he's supposed to be putting out." Drury slammed his hand on Boyle's desk and Boyle sat upright, eyes blinking. "He only gets about twenty copies printed up, doesn't distribute them to anyone."

"Where'd you get that idea?" Boyle waved away Drury's hand and scooted his chair toward the filing cabinet. "I have the invoices. He gets five hundred copies of each issue. We also pay for delivery to all the shopkeepers in Tangier."

"It's a scam."

"You have evidence?"

"Not yet." Drury drew a finger across his upper lip and clicked his tongue. "But I'll get it."

"So you decked him. Just like that. Without proof, just on a gut feeling?"

Drury nodded. "I had my reasons."

"This is a venue of the State Department. We have other ways of handling things here. For now, I'll thank you to get out of my office."

Back at his desk, Boyle picked up a pen and began writing furiously on the pad in front of him. Lily noticed he was doodling.

"Keep a close eye on Korian while we're gone," Drury said to him. "We're taking the next few days off."

He left Boyle's office, pulling Lily along behind.

Chapter Fifteen

"You don't trust Faridah. You don't trust me, your friend," Zaid was saying to MacAlistair. "But you trust a Jewish prostitute."

Suzannah was setting the table in the dining room. Adam sat in the garden with a man Lily didn't know.

"I trust you, Zaid. I trust you with my life," MacAlistair said.

"Well then—"

"It's for your own safety, Zaid. Too dangerous for you to know."

Suzannah finished at the table and left in the direction of the kitchen.

"And Suzannah? You trust her?"

"I would trust almost anyone in the mellah." MacAlistair strode toward the courtyard.

"Don't be too sure," Zaid said.

"Maybe he's right," Lily said.

Zaid gave her a grateful look. "Besides, Suzannah probably can't cook."

MacAlistair turned back and took Zaid's arm. "Of course she can. Bouillabaisse tonight. Tariq brought fresh fish when he came into town today. Couscous tomorrow." He gestured in the direction of Adam and the stranger on the patio. "Shall we wait in the garden?"

The stranger stood up with an expectant smile.

"My nephew," MacAlistair said. "Barrett Russell."

He had a trim British moustache and dark hazel eyes.

"This is Lily," MacAlistair said. "I told you about her."

The Englishman reached for Lily's hand and clasped it in both of his. "My friends call me Russ."

"Russ works in the governor's office in Gibraltar," MacAlistair said. "Comes over from time to time on government business."

"Been there since '39," Drury said. "Knows Gib inside and out."

Suzannah came back to the dining room, rosy-cheeked with the heat of the kitchen, carrying a steaming tureen of bouillabaisse. The aroma of garlic, fresh tomatoes, seafood and cilantro wafted behind her.

"Ah. I smell something fishy," Adam said.

"Fishy?" Zaid said. "What do you mean by that?"

"You people are too sensitive," Drury said, waving Zaid's words away as if he were shooing a fly.

"You people? You people?" A current of impatience emanated from Zaid, palpable, filling the garden. "To you, Berbers are animals in a zoo. You come here to observe us in our natural habitat."

Suzannah placed the tureen on the table in front of MacAlistair's setting and listened from a corner of the dining room.

"I forgot." Zaid's tone had turned to anger. "You're more interested in the Rif, the blue-eyed, blond Arabs." He added Lily to his disdain with a sweep of his arm. "Blue-eyed blondes like her are the only people you can trust, aren't they?"

Embarrassed, Lily looked away toward the dining room. Suzannah studied them, eyes narrowed in thought.

Struggling for breath, MacAlistair rasped out, "Enough, Zaid."

"More than enough," Drury said. He started into the dining room with a disgusted shrug and plopped himself into a chair.

A paroxysm of gasps and coughs wracked MacAlistair. His cheeks flushed to bright pink as he clapped a handkerchief to his mouth. Zaid rose, reached into his pocket and pulled out a fresh handkerchief.

He leaned over MacAlistair. "Sorry. So sorry." He patted MacAlistair's shoulder and handed him the handkerchief.

"The bouillabaisse grows cold," Suzannah called from the dining room. Her hand rested on Drury's shoulder.

Drury gestured to the others to join him inside. "Let's eat."

Cradling MacAlistair's arm, Zaid led his friend to his place at the head of the table and held the chair for him.

In the seat next to Lily, Russ leaned toward her and asked what she was doing in Tangier, asked how she enjoyed digging in the Caves of Hercules, asked why she became an archaeologist.

Suzannah emerged from the kitchen carrying an empty bowl. "For the bones," she said and managed to brush against Drury as she bent to set it on the table and brushed against him again when she straightened up.

She patted him on the head and slithered back to the kitchen with a wiggle. Drury's gaze followed her. Russ kept talking to Lily, and across the table, Adam watched Drury silently.

Zaid hovered over MacAlistair for the rest of the meal—as MacAlistair ladled the bouillabaisse into bowls, as they passed them around, as they piled fish bones into the basin in the middle of the table.

Before dessert, Russ told Lily, "I'd love to show you the Rock sometime. Whenever you're free."

"She has tomorrow off," Drury said from behind the mountain of bones from the bouillabaisse. "How about a day trip? Tomorrow."

They're talking in code, Lily thought. "You also work at the British Legation?" she asked Russ.

"Sometimes. I return to Gib tomorrow on the nine o'clock ferry."

"That's settled then," Drury said. "She'll meet you on the dock."

Lily looked across the table at Drury.

"It's a nice outing." Drury's head seemed to float over the basin of bones, as if he were presiding over a funeral for fish. "Ferry takes about two and a half hours."

Lily added a bone to the pile on the table.

"By the way," Drury said to MacAlistair. "Those Germans I told you about. They're getting impossible, follow us everywhere."

A glance and a nod passed between MacAlistair and Zaid, then between Zaid and Drury. That was all. But enough for Lily to understand the silent gestures.

Drury turned back to Lily and talk about Gibraltar.

"Gorham's Cave has everything. Neanderthals, Phoenicians, Carthaginians. Someday maybe you'll dig there." He looked off into the distance. "Last refuge of the Neanderthals before they vanished. From Gorham's Cave, the last Neanderthal, dying and alone, the end of his race, disappeared into the sea."

"Not quite the last Neanderthal," Adam said, with a look toward Lily and a smile at Drury.

"Russ will show you all that tomorrow," Drury told her.

"Delighted." Russ pushed back from the table and stood. "Looking forward to it." He bowed a farewell to Drury and Adam and turned to MacAlistair. "Lovely dinner. Have to get back to the British Legation." He smiled down at Lily and held out his hand. "Tomorrow morning then?"

Drury rose. "Just a minute." He signaled to Zaid. "We'll go with you. We have some business in town." Before he left the table, he said to Adam and Lily, "You young people should go up on the roof. Beautiful moon tonight," then called to Zaid, "You coming?" as he sailed out the door.

◇◇◇

Lily and Adam climbed the flight of stairs that led from the corner of the garden to the roof. Adam paused at the landing and reached into his pocket.

"They lock the door to the roof?" Lily asked.

Adam jiggled the key in the lock and turned the knob. "The moon and stars on this roof are private property. I'll show you."

Two chairs and a table sat in a shed built against the far corner of the roof, with a typewriter and radio on the table. Adam crossed to it, attached an antenna to the radio, and lifted the lid of a box next to the typewriter. Inside were two large volumes of Bureau of American Ethnology publications bound in brown cloth and a pad of graph paper.

Lily read the title. *"Ethnology of the Kwakiutl* by Franz Boas? The ethnography with a hundred and forty-seven recipes for blueberry pie? What's it doing here?"

"We bake pies."

"I see. And the typewriter?"

"The pie pan." He flipped through the pages of the top volume. "It's plugged into the transmitter and receiver over here. It's a Teletype. Messages are typed directly onto the keyboard and typed out at the other end. In code, of course. That's where the Kwakiutl come in." He opened the book. "Like this. Today is the first of November. So we open the ethnography to page 1,101—11 for November, 1 for the day of the month. The first word on the page is *matrilineal."* He sat at the table and reached for the graph paper. "So we make a chart in which *m,* the first letter, equals *a*; *a,* the second, equals *b*; and so on." He began to fill out squares on the pad, writing the alphabet along the top line, then *m, a,* and *t* under the first three letters.

Lily looked over his shoulder. "I see. *R* becomes *d.* What happens when you get to the second occurrence of the *r,* or the *a,* for that matter?"

"Ignore it and keep on going."

"And if all twenty-six letters aren't on that page?"

"Just use the regular letters of the alphabet for the tail end. Here, try it."

Lily sat down at the table and moved the book toward her. She picked up the pencil and, reading down the page, filled in the rest of the alphabet.

"Seems pretty simplistic to me. Like the code ring you get in a box of cereal. Isn't there a better way?"

"In the Pacific, they send messages in Navaho. We can't do that in the European Theater. German linguists run the codes. Some of them are experts in American Indian languages. The Brits use a method similar to this, but they use *Rebecca.* The trick is to change the code every day."

"*Rebecca*? The novel?"

Adam nodded. "The Germans use a complicated machine for their code, Enigma. It's more direct, already encrypted into the Teletype. They change the code every day, but there are a limited number of permutations."

"What happens if someone finds the code book?"

"Then we might be in trouble—if they can figure out Drury's convoluted thinking."

"Now that we have today's code, how do we send a message?"

"Just turn on the radio, this switch to receive, this one to transmit. Mostly, when you operate this, you'll be relaying messages between Gibraltar and Casablanca. We use FM bands. They have a shorter range. That's why we have to relay. But FM is more secure. The Krauts use regular AM bands, not FM, so there's less chance of their intercepting us."

"Why?"

"No more questions. You'll understand it better tomorrow, after you go to Gib."

He picked up the paper she had written on, tore it into small pieces, and dropped them in a large brass ashtray.

He pulled a Zippo lighter from his pocket and set the scraps of paper afire. "Afterward, you burn the notes." He waited while the paper flared up. "Crumble them when they're finished burning. Sometimes there's a palimpsest from writing on charred paper."

When the flames died out, he stirred the brittle black snippets with the tip of a pencil. "And make sure it's out, that there are no sparks, especially if there's a wind. We don't want to set the house on fire by mistake."

He pocketed the lighter and pulled out a set of car keys. "I'll drive you home. Zaid is busy tonight."

Lily slept in spurts, wondering about Gibraltar, letters and codes weaving through her waking thoughts.

In the morning, Lily noticed that the Germans were not waiting for her when she left the hotel.

Chapter Sixteen

"Gateway to the Mediterranean," Russ said. "Whoever controls the Rock controls the underbelly of Europe." The limestone cliffs of Gibraltar loomed in front of them. "This is where the Berbers under Tariq ibn Ziyad swept into Andalusia when the Moors conquered Spain."

"And Moulay Yousef's brave soldiers brought peace and Allah to the Iberian continent," Lily said, imitating the Mekraj's voice, reciting his extraordinary version of history.

Russ looked puzzled. "Indeed. The Moroccans named the mountain after ibn Ziyad, called it Jebal al Tariq. Hence, Gibraltar."

The ferry cruised nearer and nearer to the rocky silhouette outlined against the sky.

"The Rock is one of the Pillars of Hercules. The other is Jebal Musa on the Moroccan side of the Strait, near Cuesta."

"There's a Jebel Musa in Moab," Lily said. "Near Petra."

"No relation. Hercules himself set up this pair of mountains as the gateway to the Great Ocean."

"And beyond here was the end of the world," Lily said.

For a moment she could believe it, could see the curve of the earth along the horizon, falling off to oblivion.

"In the Miocene, there was a land bridge here between Europe and Africa."

"Beg pardon?"

"Before the Ice Ages. The Mediterranean was two vast, land-locked lakes, the sea level lower, with high rates of evaporation. Africa and Europe were connected here. Also further east, from Tunisia to Sicily."

Russ continued to stare at her.

"It was a different world then." She tried to imagine it. A world without people, just the primitive ancestors of the animals we know today. "Eventually the limestone rock eroded, the Atlantic spilled in and swirled around the Pillars."

"And you were there?" Russ asked. He faced her, looked at her intently. "You're frightened, aren't you?"

"A little. Should I be?"

"Sometimes. Not today."

The ferry swerved with a light breeze and the sea surged around the base of the Rock.

"It looks like a lion, crouched for the kill," Lily said.

"It is. The cliffs are pockmarked with gun emplacements." Russ squinted into the sun. "Can you make out the cannons?"

Closer in, the ferry negotiated around warships assembled for maneuvers inside the moles that formed the harbor. "The light-colored ones are from the Mediterranean fleet," Russ told her. "Dark ones are local."

They moved slowly into the dock, to a bustling English presence. British Tommies in khaki and jack tars, lorries, noisy machine shops, all crowded the pier.

"We have everything we need right here on our little island. Restaurants, cinema, pubs, good shops—and palm trees. We even have a racecourse. No need to travel out of the colony. English village life and a Mediterranean climate. The best of both worlds."

With a grandiose gesture he swept his arms toward palm trees, tile-roofed houses with their geranium window boxes rising along the hill. "It's the stepping stone to the Orient, with afternoon teas and red phone booths, Union Jacks and Barbary apes."

A file of blue-helmeted Bobbies marched along the palmetto-lined esplanade toward the town.

"They're on the lookout for spies?" she asked.

"Just keeping the peace."

A tawny furred creature leaped from the roof of a car to the brick pavement.

"A Barbary ape." Lily pointed. "There, behind the taxi." She turned to Russ. "They're not apes, you know. Tailless monkeys, the only ones in Europe. Besides humans, of course."

"You'll see more on Ape's Rock in the center of the peninsula," Russ said. "We say that Gibraltar will remain British as long as Barbary apes live on the Rock."

A member of the crew bounded onto the dock to secure the ferry. Lily and Russ moved along the gangplank while bundles of netted cargo swung above their heads. Involuntarily, Lily ducked.

Murky water, dotted with orange peels, slapped against the keel and the gangplank swayed.

Russ watched her from the dock. "Don't have on your sea legs today?" He held out a hand. "Jump."

Lily balled her fists, her arms stiff against her sides, and hurtled onto the dock.

They took a taxi into town along narrow streets through a jumble of houses scattered against the lower slopes, passing carts on squeaky wheels that competed for space in the cramped lanes.

The sleepy little town contrasted with the lazy bustle of Tangier. Neat gardens surrounded cottages; doors trimmed with polished brass caught the glare of late morning; shutters garnished the sun-drenched brightness of walls. Ahead of them, a man carried a basket of bread on his shoulder, trudging uphill.

And over it all, the Rock.

The taxi stopped at Casemate Square at the entrance to Main Street. Russ gestured toward a company of Scottish guards in green and yellow tartans lined up in formation before Government House.

"Gordon Highlanders," he said. "We're safe here on the Rock. Don't let the kilts fool you. They're brave and bloodthirsty. We call them the Ladies from Hell."

They hiked up through the narrow streets of the town, climbing higher and higher, following a path along the hill.

"This the way to Gorham's Cave?" Lily asked.

"That was just window dressing. We're going to the Northern Tunnels."

"To meet Drury?"

"No. He's at HQ this morning, in Dockyard tunnel."

"Where?"

"HQ. Eisenhower is managing the whole operation from headquarters set up in the tunnels at the far western end of Gib. Drury has to be back in Tangier this afternoon. Came in on the early ferry. We have other work to do."

"Such as?"

"You'll see when you get there." Russ continued up the hill. "You coming?"

Lily puffed up the incline after him, still curious and a little resentful about the lack of explanation. She paused when she spotted a monkey sitting on a high rock, nursing a baby folded in the crook of her arm. The infant waved its legs in the air and clutched at its mother's fur.

Russ maneuvered along a path marked with cart tracks and along the hill to an arched cleft cut into the rock. She turned away from the Barbary apes and trudged after him.

A Highlander at the opening in the rock watched their approach. He moved aside, shifting the bayonet smartly to his left shoulder, and saluted.

"You'll come with us, Peters," Russ said.

"I've been waiting, sir."

They entered a passageway eight feet high and just as wide hewn into the rock. The Highlander followed. The deafening bray of a donkey reverberated through the gallery.

Russ pulled a flashlight from his pocket. "We dug out the Northern Tunnels during the Great Siege. It was the only way we could transport the guns to set up a battery on the steep northern face of the Rock."

"The Great Siege?"

"In the eighteenth century. While you Yanks were fighting us in your Revolution, the Spanish and French took advantage of our distraction and surrounded the Rock. Eventually, we prevailed." Lily followed the eerie echo of his voice. "In spite of scurvy, starvation, constant bombardment."

The beam from Russ' lantern bounced off the walls. A fusty animal odor permeated the clammy air.

"There's a lesson there," he said. "Hitler should take it to heart."

They picked their way over the slippery limestone floor, past side rooms and stone staircases into a connecting passageway.

A hobbled donkey wearing a burlap sack tied under the tail to catch its droppings was hitched to a cart that blocked the narrow passage. Behind it, light moved back and forth through an aperture cut into the rock. A sign over the opening read "Hanover Gallery 1789".

A resounding voice rumbled out, "In here."

They squeezed around the donkey cart into a small chamber hacked out of the rock. Wooden boxes were stacked against the walls of the gallery, some the size of fruit crates, some as large as coffins. One had been pried open.

Adam was wearing a headlamp and jamming Enfield rifles and straw into a gunnysack stamped with a Union Jack and the legend OFFICIAL BUSINESS.

He bent over it, his head tilted at an awkward angle, his khaki shirt smudged, his face streaked with dust and sweat.

"Welcome to my lair," Adam said.

Chapter Seventeen

Adam handed Lily a rifle. Her arm strained at its unexpected weight.

Startled, she almost dropped it. "What's this for?"

"We're filling those sacks." He pointed with his chin to a stack of bags against the far wall. "They go to Tangier in the diplomatic pouch on the afternoon ferry." He stuffed another gun into the canvas bag.

Lily eyed the clutch of filled sacks arrayed near the entrance to the chamber. "That's all we do?" She leaned the rifle against the wall and reached for a bag.

"Nothing too difficult," Adam said. "You and I fill. Russ, here, seals. Sergeant Peters, outside, loads them onto a cart to transfer to a lorry."

She held open the sack with her right hand. Adam watched as she picked up the rifle and tried to jam it into the bag. The gun slipped out of her hand and clattered to the floor.

"Never mind," Adam said. He exchanged her rifle for a crowbar. "Start on the ammo instead. Over there by the far wall."

Russ had already started working. Squatting on the ground, he tied the opening of a bag crammed with guns, melted a bit of red wax onto a flap folded over the twine, and stamped it with a bulky seal.

Lily pried open the case.

"Those are 30-06's for the Einfields," Adam told her. "Take them out of the ammo case. They come sealed twenty to a box."

"Why are we doing this?" Lily asked him.

"Drury didn't brief you?"

She shook her head.

"These go in the British diplomatic pouch to Tangier. From Tangier, you'll get them to Tariq. He'll deliver them to the Merkaj to distribute to the Berber. They're our backup in case the landings in Casa go sour and Spanish step in or the Vichy French put up too much resistance."

"As regular troops?"

"Guerillas."

"How do I get them to Tariq?"

"Tomorrow," Adam said and shoved a rifle into the open sack.

They worked in silence, the smell of metal and oil and gelignite permeating the stagnant air of the cavern. Lily and Adam stuffed bags and Russ sealed them. Peters hoisted the sacks onto his shoulders. Red-faced and grunting with effort, he carried them out of the chamber.

After a while, Lily developed a rhythm. She moved a pile of sacks to the case, held the open bag in her left hand and reached in to grab a box of ammo with her right. One after the other, in endless movement.

They stopped for egg sandwiches at two, sitting on the ground in the clammy chamber, leaning their backs against the wall. After a fifteen-minute break, Peters rummaged in the food hamper for an apple. "For the donkey," he said and disappeared into the tunnel.

By mid-afternoon, Lily's shoulders ached. She rested, squatting on her heels. The others looked as tired as she felt, but kept working steadily, filling sacks, sealing them, carrying them out.

She picked up the crowbar and opened another crate.

When they finally finished, Lily, Adam, and Russ started back down the tunnel while Peters stayed behind to load the remaining sacks onto the cart.

The fetid air in the tunnel stuck in Lily's throat. Sweat rolled down the small of her back. She couldn't remember being this tired since she was an undergraduate working the rocker screen at a Folsom site in Idaho.

A rumble of cartwheels on the stone floor of the tunnel and the clip-clop of the mule sounded behind them.

"Coming through," Peters called.

They flattened themselves against the wall until the cart passed and resumed walking single file through the tunnel, Russ taking the lead, with Lily right behind him.

"When you get back on the ferry, you'll see Sergeant Peters drive a lorry onto the dock." Russ' voice carried back to her with an echo. "He'll leave it there to be loaded onto the ferry. Don't show any sign you know him."

"What do I do?"

"Watch from the deck. See that it's loaded without incident. Don't go near the lorry, not the ramp, not the hold. But keep your eyes open for anything unusual."

"Such as?"

"Any incident. Someone taking special notice, nervous, paying too much attention. Report it back to us."

"You won't be coming back on the ferry?"

He shook his head no. "Someone from the British Legation will be on the dock at Tangier. Engage him in casual conversation if you see anything suspicious."

"How will I know him?"

"You know the British," Adam said. "Probably bowler hat, furled umbrella."

Russ turned around, harrumphed at Adam, then continued down the tunnel. "Red hair, horned rim glasses, red moustache, about five foot ten, weighs about eleven stone six."

"What?"

"About one hundred sixty pounds," Adam said from behind. "A stone is the equivalent of fourteen pounds."

Russ turned around again. "Sorry. Forgot you don't speak English in the colonies."

"And if there's an emergency?" Lily asked.

"You're on your own."

Lily glanced back at Adam for reassurance.

"Probably won't be one," Adam said. "If there is, the hell with the guns. Take care of your own safety." He looked weary. "You'll be all right." He drew a handkerchief across his face and wiped his hands. "Tomorrow morning you're expected at the villa at 9:30."

"You'll be there?"

"No. MacAlistair will fill you in."

They parted at the entrance to the tunnel. A sharp intake of breath filled Lily's lungs with the cool afternoon air. She found her way back to the ferry along the path that led downhill into the town, cradling her arms across her chest against the breeze. She stumbled, unsure of her direction, looking for landmarks, then continued downhill, through the town, past the houses, to the dock.

On the ferry, cold gusts swirled around Lily, blowing her hair against her face. She watched the dock from the rail, hunching her shoulders and clutching her arms against the chill wind. Crates dangled from a crane and swung back and forth like pendulums as they were lowered toward a ramp that led to the hold.

Peters appeared in a white van that pulled up short of the ramp. He handed the captain some papers attached to a clipboard. The captain signed while gusts whipped at Peters' kilt. Lily smiled, remembering his answer to the old question, "What do you wear under—?"

"My knees," he had answered before she finished the question.

Two Moroccan women, heads covered by scarves, lumbered up the gangplank. A pretty girl teetering on platform shoes with ankle straps slithered behind them in a tight skirt, her black hair piled high on top of her head. One of the women struggled with her cloth bundle to retie it while the girl stood at the cabin door, tapping her foot and motioning the woman inside.

Struggling against the wind, the captain removed some papers and returned the clipboard to Peters. Peters started toward town, the board tucked under his right arm.

Lily held her breath as the crane lifted the van. It lurched precariously in the wind, hovered over the dock, nose down, and wavered over the ferry. Three deck hands scrambled out of the hold, loosened the chains that held the van, lowered it and guided it along the ramp into the cargo door.

Chilled, she rubbed her arms and moved inside. The salon was almost empty. A swarthy man in a dark suit read a Spanish language newspaper, half a page folded back in a commuter's pleat. From time to time he glanced over the top of the paper at the girl, who paraded around the salon, heels clicking on the wooden floor. The two women sat close together, bundles clutched on their laps.

The ferry vibrated to a start, engines rumbling in the bowels of the hold. By the time it pulled away from the dock, the girl was at the coffee bar and flirting with the steward in a low voice, her elbow leaning on the bar and a coquettish tilt to her head. Beyond the shelter of the harbor moles, the boat began to roll and heave in the wind-swept water, wider and wider. Lily watched the Rock recede through the spray-specked windows of the salon.

The boat swayed with the thrashing currents where a furious ocean funneled through the Straits, and she heard noises coming from below the deck, first a creaking, then a rolling sound. The ferry pitched in earnest now, as though it were being tossed in an angry fist. The clatter from the hold grew louder, metal scudding across metal, reverberating with the sway of the boat.

Lily left the musty cabin for the deck. The door swung back and forth and snapped against the jamb with a hollow click. One of the Moroccan women ran past her from the salon, leaned over the rail and retched.

Lily moved away. She craned her neck to scan the upper deck. The captain emerged from the wheelhouse, took off his cap, wiped his forehead and studied the gathering clouds. He jammed the cap back on his forehead and stood with his legs apart and his hands behind his back, riding the swells, a pair of wire spectacles sliding down the bridge of his nose.

Lily climbed the narrow stairs, clutching the banister to maintain a precarious balance. She swayed and held on while the wind whipped against her skirt. The ferry heaved against a swell. She smashed against the metal of the stair.

Her stocking caught on the rough surface of the wall and snagged. Damn. Her last unmended pair.

When she reached the upper deck, she smoothed her skirt, held it down against the wind, and grasped the rail with the other.

As casually as she could, she nodded at the captain and gave him a tentative smile. "Rough sea."

"A Levanter," he said. "Wind out of the east. Nothing to worry about."

Lily glanced below. The Moroccan woman still leaned over the rail. "Not many passengers."

"It's the war," the captain said, "the time of year. In summer, a few people cross over from Gib to Morocco for the beaches. But mostly, Spaniards go out of Algeciras to Cuesta."

"It hardly pays for you to make the trip."

"We have cargo."

"Is that what's making the noise down below?"

The captain removed his water-spotted spectacles and wiped them with a handkerchief. "Not much cargo today. Just some mail, office equipment, the diplomatic pouch."

"Anything ever damaged in the swells?" Lily asked. "It sounds like things are crashing around down there."

He replaced his glasses, rolling one earpiece in place at a time. "Loose chains. We use them to hold cargo in place. The empty ones roll about a bit."

He sniffed the air. "Weather's changing." He pointed overhead to a bevy of storks swooping over the Straits. "They're carried by the wind. Winter over in Africa."

He adjusted his jacket and, with a curt nod to Lily, strolled back to the wheelhouse.

When Lily returned to the lower deck, the Moroccan woman had already let go of the rail and tottered back to the salon. The women and the girl sat pale and hollow-eyed, clutching the edges of their seats. Lily felt queasy herself. The man was asleep, his head tilted against the top of his chest. Soft sounds, halfway between a snore and a gasp rasped from his open mouth.

Lily lingered on the deck in Tangier while the cargo was unloaded. The women disembarked, waddled along the quay, and disappeared through the gate of the medina. The man with the newspaper loitered on the pier. He scrutinized each passerby, watching whoever came out of the medina. He seemed to be interested in the cargo.

A proper Englishman appeared—a three-piece suit, red hair, horned rim glasses, red moustache. And he carried a furled umbrella.

Lily started down the ramp as she watched the man with the newspaper continue to scan the pier. What will I say to the Englishman? Nice day, I'll say. Look out for the man with the newspaper, I'll say, he's loitering.

The man with the newspaper turned to stare at the English-man and then looked past him to a bearded man carrying a briefcase and wearing a dark brown djelaba. The man with the newspaper waved, greeted the bearded man with a peck on each cheek, and they vanished into the medina arm in arm.

The Englishman signed the clipboard the captain handed him. Just before he got into the van and drove off, Lily spotted Korian on the pier near the newspaper kiosk. What's he doing here?

Korian picked up a paper, dug into his pocket, and dropped some coins on the counter. Lily started down the gangplank. Korian hesitated a moment, silhouetted by the setting sun. A man in a dark blue suit appeared next to him. As Korian reached out to shake the man's hand, she saw something pass between them.

Before the man moved on, he slid a small package into Korian's pocket.

Korian stayed at the kiosk for a few moments, scanning the headlines, turning the paper to read the bottom half of the page, and then strode off.

What had they exchanged?

Lily hurried to follow Korian through the clattering industry of the dock, squinting after him in the glare of sunset, plunging into the hazy twilight and busy noise of the medina.

She lost sight of him somewhere around the Rue d'Angleterre where he seemed to disappear.

Wherever he's going, I'll catch him later, find out what's going on.

She bent her head into the wind that pricked at her ears and she trudged on in the direction of the Legation.

Lily saw no one in the hall. A sliver of light leaked through the bottom of her closed office door. She moved quietly down the corridor and thrust the door open, expecting to surprise Korian rummaging through her desk again.

Instead, she found Drury and Suzannah clinging to each other, Drury's arms clasping Suzannah in an embrace, Suzannah's head resting on his shoulder.

They jumped apart when Lily opened the door. Suzannah gasped. Her hands flew to her face and she ran past Lily and down the corridor.

Lily took in her breath and stepped into the office. "She's been crying?"

Drury nodded.

"What…?"

"I don't want to talk about it. Let's give her time to leave, then we'll go," he said.

"You don't want to be seen together?"

He nodded again.

Lily waited until they were in the street before she asked more. "About Suzannah—"

Drury stiffened. "What about Suzannah?"

"Be careful with her. I saw her in the Ville Nouvelle the other day."

"So?" He walked rapidly away, down the hill and into the crowded street.

"She was with a Spanish officer." Lily had to run to keep up with him.

"Let it go. You don't know anything about her."

They were at the Petite Socco now. "I don't think you can trust her," Lily said.

"It's none of your business." His hands were in his pockets and he backed away. "I told you, you don't know anything about her."

Patrons in the small café next to them put down their glasses of tea, intent on the argument unfolding in front of them.

"You're shouting."

"Shouting? I'll do more than that."

Lily avoided the stares of the street urchins who had stopped begging for change.

"People are looking at us."

"I don't give a damn if God is looking at us with pink-eye."

Lily gestured toward the café behind him, toward the specta-tors watching from their tables. "Careful, Drury!"

But he wouldn't stop. "Don't tell me who to trust and not to trust." He was shouting now, red-faced, the cords on his neck stretching and beating. "What do you know about what she does?

"You're making a scene. Everyone can hear us argue."

He opened his mouth to speak, then turned away. With his hands balled in his pockets, Drury trudged toward where Zaid was waiting in the Hillman.

"You sure you know what you're doing?" Lily called after him.

Drury reached the car and got into the front seat next to Zaid. They waited in silence until Lily clambered into the back.

"Got carried away," Drury said, and was silent for the rest of the drive up The Mountain.

Chapter Eighteen

In the morning, Lily took the bus up to the villa to see MacAlistair. She checked her watch. It was precisely nine thirty.

She squeezed past a pickup truck loaded with oranges parked in the drive and rang the bell. She could hear Zaid's voice echoing through the courtyard.

MacAlistair opened the door. He led her into a side room with a black and white tiled floor, a desk, and a mirror from Marrakech with an elaborate lacquered frame canted on the wall.

Zaid followed. "I could take care of it, you know," he said. "No need to send someone else."

"I need you here," MacAlistair answered. He turned to Lily. "You're to drive to Asilah. There's a lorry just outside in the driveway. The material you are to transport is in the bed of the lorry covered by a load of oranges." He spread a map on the desk. "You know where Asilah is? It's a little fishing village down the coast."

"I went once with Drury. We were on the way to Lixus."

"The Roman site?"

Lily nodded. "Roman, Phoenician. Where Hercules went for the golden apples."

"If you get to Lixus, you've gone too far."

Zaid stood watching them, his arms crossed across his chest, his face a mask of impatience. Lily tried smiling at him, tried making a joke about the golden apples being a load of oranges. Zaid remained stony-faced.

MacAlistair coughed lightly and picked up a pen. "Let's stay on topic." He traced a route from Tangier to Asilah with the pen. "The coastal road is off limits. You have to go inland." He began to cough again and paused for breath. "Keep a log of how long it takes to get to each point, any strange activities or installations along the way."

Zaid was watching Lily with half-closed eyes. "Too complicated for her."

"All I have to do is follow the route, keep a log. How complicated is that?"

"You have to keep a log of the road, note to the tenth of a mile on the speedometer all cuts, banks, overhangs, culverts, bridges. Also the position of Spanish defenses."

"Drive with one hand and write it all down with the other?"

MacAlistair looked at Lily over the rim of his glasses. "You'll manage. Take it slowly." He folded the map and handed it to Lily. "You'll find a restaurant, the Casa Pépé, in Asilah."

"I know the place."

"Fishermen moor their boats at the foot of that street. Park the lorry there, next to the sea wall. Leave the keys under the seat and meet Adam at the restaurant at noon."

Zaid shifted from one foot to another. "You sure you can do this?"

"Certainly."

He turned to MacAlistair. "Suppose someone from the Guardia Civil stops her? What will she do?"

"She'll think of something."

"In this part of the world, women don't drive lorries," Zaid said.

MacAlistair contemplated Lily, went to a cupboard on the far wall and took out a dark djelaba. "Wear this. It's for a man." He turned it over and pointed to a tassel sewn at the tip of the pointed hood. "See this? Men wear them with tassels, women don't. Tie your hair back and pull up the hood. When you're finished, leave it on the passenger seat."

He started toward the door. "I'll get the keys to the lorry."

Zaid examined her again, sighed, and followed MacAlistair out.

Zaid's voice still rung through the house as she pulled the djelaba over her clothes, found a rubber band on the desk and tied back her hair. She raised the hood and looked into the mirror.

Only the dark pointed hood of the djelaba was visible.

Faceless, eyes hidden in the deep shadows of the hood, someone nameless stood before her, remote and menacing.

"My God! I look like the Angel of Death," Lily said from the hollow of the garment.

Over her shoulder, she saw MacAlistair, pale, mouth agape, studying her.

MacAlistair cleared his throat. "You only are who you think you are." He held out the keys.

Chapter Nineteen

The inland route MacAlistair had marked was less a road than a dirt track that ran from village to village, first veering to the southeast, then to the west. Lily would watch the route, glance at her watch, and scribble notes on the pad that she had placed on the seat next to her.

She stalled behind donkey carts that clogged the way as they carried produce to a Tuesday market. Off to the side the market spread across an open field pocked with scattered sheep, tethered cows, two horses, and farmers selling from their carts.

Just past the town, a policeman from the Guardia Civil blocked the road. Lily pushed the map and notepad behind her and sank deeper into the hood of the djelaba, trying to conceal her face in its shadow. She slowed when the policeman flagged her down.

He barked something at her in the rapid, guttural lisp of Madrid. She barely understood every third word.

"Bismillah," she muttered in a deep voice from depths of the hood.

He paused, took a breath, and spoke again in Spanish, slower and louder with elaborate gestures, as if she were deaf. He seemed to be saying that the road ahead was closed because of an airfield.

Lily nodded. *"Gracias, shukran,"* she said and pulled away in the direction he was pointing. She glanced in the rearview mirror to see him look after her and turn away with a disgusted shrug.

She bumped eastward along the side of the rutted track, passing carts going in the other direction toward the market. When she was well beyond detection by the policeman, she retrieved the notepad and turned southwest again toward Asilah.

By noon she knew from the salt smell of the air and the freshening breeze that she neared the sea. Ahead she could just make out the Portuguese ramparts encircling Asilah's medina. The trip, no more than thirty miles, had taken a little more than two hours.

Casa Pépé was across from a grove of twisted oaks outside the walls of the medina. She drove past the restaurant, parking near the little harbor at the foot of the street. She hid the keys and map under the seat and climbed out of the cab of the pickup.

The djelaba swirled in the cold November wind. Lily kept it on, shivering and wrapped it around her as the hood loosened and fell across her shoulders. With the hood down and her hair untied, she hoped no one would notice the tassel at the point of the hood.

Gloomy clouds hovered over the fishing boats anchored in the gray, choppy sea. Empty boats, their sails furled, bobbled in scruffy water that smelled of dead fish. Farther down along the harbor, a Riffian sat huddled in a donkey cart laden with fish.

Adam waited just inside the door of the restaurant, out of the wind. "Any trouble finding the place?"

"Not really. I was here before with Drury."

They sat at an inside table facing the street, their fingers wound around warming bowls of thick soup, and ordered civelles—baby elvers, no bigger than matchsticks—sautéed in butter and garlic.

"When you came here with Drury…." Adam's voice trailed off as he watched the street through the restaurant window.

"We came for the antiquities. A friend of Drury's dug a burial mound with standing stones near here about seven years ago. Not much left. Just a few holes in the ground."

Adam nodded. He tilted toward the window, his eyes straining in the direction of the harbor.

"We went to Lixus, too," she went on, filling the silence. "Carthaginians had a thriving fish-salting industry there. You can still see the storage vats and cisterns."

Lily heard the door of the pickup slam, saw it drive away. The donkey cart was gone now.

"Asilah was once the ancient Phoenician city of Silis," she went on. "In Roman times, it was famous for garum, shipped all over the empire from here."

"Garum?"

"A fish sauce made of anchovies, with a notorious smell. Romans considered it a delicacy."

"Like Worcestershire sauce?"

"Stronger. And smellier."

Adam shrugged and took another forkful of the eels. "Different countries, different customs." He glanced at the street again.

Lily waited for him to say more. He didn't. "Romans influenced everything in Morocco." She watched him scan the harbor and kept talking. "Not just the ruins at Volubilis. Moroccan houses have rooms with divans running along three walls and open to a courtyard. That's taken from the Roman house plan." *I'm babbling nonsense.* "And the dining rooms—*triclinia*—had divans along the walls like Moroccan houses." She didn't know if he was listening. "Romans ate reclining on the divans."

"Dipping their fish in smelly garum?"

He did hear her.

"Exactly."

The waiter brought a dish of tangerines. Adam reached for one and continued to gaze out the window.

"Are we waiting for something?"

"It'll be a while," he said.

"We could go for a walk."

"I suppose." He asked for the bill, counted out some pesetas, and rose, pushing back the chair. "Shall we?"

They sauntered through quiet streets in the whitewashed medina and out toward the sea through the Sea Gate, the Bab el Bahar, along a path lined with black anchors that followed the shore.

They strolled along a beach that seemed to stretch for miles. It was low tide. At the edge of the water, dead starfish curled on the damp sand.

Passing a mass of jagged rocks where an unforgiving sea foamed and crashed, Lily gestured toward a tower that hovered over them.

"That's the palace of Raisuli the Brigand, the infamous pasha. He once held an American citizen captive for ransom. Teddy Roosevelt sent gunboats to the rescue." She pointed to a high window above. "Raisuli forced his enemies to jump from that window onto the rocks."

I'm chattering again. What's wrong with me?

Adam looked up. "Pretty steep fall."

"They say one of his victims cried out as he died that the rocks were more merciful than Raisuli."

"What happened to him?"

"Raisuli? He released the so-called American, who turned out to be Greek. Roosevelt won the election, and according to Drury, Raisuli was finally captured by Abd el Krim."

Beyond the rocks, a dark sea roiled and surged like an angry serpent. Wincing from the cold blasts that thrashed over the water, Lily huddled deeper into the warmth of the djelaba.

"We'd better get back," Adam said.

They sat at one of the outside tables at Casa Pépé. Adam ordered hot tea and cornes de gazelle—tiny crescents stuffed with almonds and honey and rolled in sugar and chopped nuts.

Lily wrapped her hands around the tea glass to warm them, while Adam watched the street.

A radio played inside the restaurant and the sound filtered out to them, the melancholy whine of ancient instruments: the hoarse tones of the kamanche, its curved horsehair bow scraping across the strings, the sensuous cadence of the long-necked oud, the seductive, shrill measures of the flute. She felt the music, the wild excitement of the tambour drums, fingers singing, beating, pulsing, eddying into her soul.

Across from her, Adam's hands danced on the edge of the table. Their eyes held. They swayed, bent, clapped, swirled together in time to the music.

The music stopped and they both laughed.

After an awkward pause, Adam took a small jewelry box from his tunic. "I bought you something."

Flushing, Lily put down the tea and opened the box to find a silver filigree pendant shaped like a hand and set with a garnet.

"It keeps away the evil eye," Adam said. "It's a charm to ward off danger, a hamsa, the Hand of Fatima."

Lily held up the hamsa by the chain, then put it in her palm and fingered the silver filigree. She turned it to the light, admiring the rich, deep red of the garnet. "I don't think I should accept this. I'm involved with someone, you know."

"A prior commitment?"

Lily nodded. "You could say that."

"Your friend in the Hagannah? Someone with the British Eighth Army?"

"How did you know?"

"You asked me a lot of questions about the Eighth Army. British? Palestinian?"

Lily shook her head. "American."

"You haven't heard from him?"

"Rafi doesn't know where I am."

"Rafi?" Adam looked away. "There was an American attached to the British Eighth Army, Ralph Landon. We called him Rafi." He swallowed. He seemed about to say something more, but stopped.

"You know him?" Lily asked.

Inside, the radio was still playing, voices now, garbled and indistinct. It switched off and silence lay between them.

"I met him in Tobruk," Adam said.

"Where is he? I have to write him. Rafi doesn't know I'm in North Africa, probably thinks I'm still in Chicago." She stopped.

A dark wind swirled across her shoulder and ran down her spine like a winding sheet. "He's in Tobruk?"

Clouds glowered in the murky sky. Adam hesitated, scanning Lily's face, and reached for her hand.

"I'm sorry," Adam said.

Lily felt a dizzying chill, the blood drain from her face. She turned away, watching the leaves eddy in peevish gusts as they scudded along the road.

"Sorry? About what?"

Adam took a deep breath. "On the eve of Rommel's attack in the second battle of El Alemein," he began, "Rafi made a phony map with details of a counterfeit minefield and desert hazards, then drove out to the desert in an armored car. He faked a breakdown near the German lines and abandoned the car and map."

"That's like him, you know."

Adam nodded and patted Lily's hand. "The ruse worked. Rommel took the route we wanted him to, drove his tanks through a real minefield. We were able to pin down the Twelfth and Fifteenth Panzer divisions."

The wind off the harbor carried a stench of the rotted debris of low tide. Lily couldn't look at Adam. She didn't want to hear the rest. She traced the pattern on the oilcloth with her fingers as one fat raindrop splattered on the table, then another.

"And Rafi?"

"He…." Adam cleared his throat. "Rafi was caught in the crossfire in the German minefield."

"He's wounded?" Her eyes stung, her vision warped with brimming tears. "In a hospital? Where?"

"He…." Adam shook his head. "He didn't make it."

The hamsa fell from Lily's hand. Adam reached into his pocket and handed Lily a handkerchief.

He picked up the charm and held it by the chain, his eyes still on Lily. "He did what he had to do. Rafi's sacrifice turned the tide against Rommel."

The damp air held the smell of rain. Heavy clouds lumbered across the sky. A few drops spotted the table.

Adam pushed back his chair and stood up, the hamsa dangling from his hand as he came around behind Lily and patted her shoulder. "Rafi would want you to have this." He clasped the chain around her neck. "A charm to keep you safe," he said. "Think of it as a gift from Rafi."

Lily stared at the darkened sky. Across the way, palm trees worried in the wind. At the foot of the street, fishing boats tossed in the angry water of the harbor, their masts rocking and angling. Raindrops puddled on the oilcloth of the table.

Tariq passed. Without stopping, he dropped the keys of the truck next to Adam's plate.

Rain fell in earnest now, washing away motes of dust, streaming over the backs of chairs. She sat in the downpour.

Adam pulled her to her feet. "Let's get out of here." He threw some money on the table. "It's coming down in buckets."

He held her by the elbow as they ran to the pickup parked at the foot of the street, through furious spates of rain sweeping over them like a curtain, through water splashing over the tips of their shoes.

Her skirt smelled of wet wool and was heavy with rain. It flapped against her legs as she climbed into the cab of the pickup.

Adam wiped condensation from the windshield with the edge of his sleeve. "This better clear up. God knows what they'll do if the storm continues. They can't hang off the coast forever." Adam narrowed his eyes, peering at the water-veiled window. "They're green troops. Came directly across the Atlantic from the States." He fished for the keys. "Some of them straight out of school."

Lily turned to him. He had started the truck and was backing up, looking over his shoulder. "What are you talking about?" she asked.

"Operation Torch."

"Oh." Operation Torch. Of course.

They drove into heavy rain sheeting against the glass. Her feet were cold and wet. "About Torch. They can't go through Gibraltar, you know." She was shivering. "U-boats are lying off Cape Spartel."

"Not any more, they're not. Drury and MacAlistair leaked the news that we're preparing an invasion of Belgium. Tariq tells me the U-boats are gone. Further north in the Atlantic, probably. Allied task forces can pass through starting tomorrow."

The rain coursed over the windshield and down the hood of the truck. Tears from the sky. Even God is crying.

Lily sat frozen, staring at the windshield. *Maybe Rafi is just missing.*

"You didn't see it yourself," Lily said. "You don't really know if he's dead."

The incessant click-clack of the wipers nodding back and forth like a metronome hypnotized her and overwhelmed her with a visceral sadness.

"I saw him when…." He glanced at her, then peered through the foggy window. "When they brought him in."

They hit a depression in the road. Water spurted against the windows of the truck and Adam rode the brakes. "We'll come in on the Atlantic side, near Casablanca. Three landings in all, the one in Morocco, one at Oran, and one east of Algiers."

Rafi dead? That can't be true. Why is the war going on without him? "If we had gotten married sooner instead of waiting to finish my dissertation," Lily said, "if we had had a child…."

"It's time to let Boyle in on it," Adam said. "Even de Gaulle doesn't know about Operation Torch yet. Won't know 'til D minus one."

"There's nothing left of him," Lily said aloud. "It's as though he never lived."

"Rafi? His action made all the difference. Two Panzer divisions were put out of action. We owe the success at El Alemein to him. Always remember, he saved the day." Adam glanced at her and looked back at the road, squinting through the rain. "Thanks to Rafi, the Brits are on the ground in the Western Desert. They plan to move west against Rommel so we can catch him in a pincer movement. They'll have their hands full. We have to hope that Spain maintains her neutrality, that the Krauts won't move through Spain to Gibraltar."

They drove in silence, listening to the steady clip clop of the wipers.

"Who did they leak it to?" Lily asked after a while.

"What? Oh, the story about the invasion of Belgium." Adam shrugged, splaying out his hands on the steering wheel. "Could be anyone. Whatever they did, it worked."

"Was it Korian?"

"I'm not sure."

They fell silent again. Adam maneuvered the pickup through the rain. Mud exploded against the window as the truck bounced over a rut. Instinctively, Lily ducked.

"Careful around here," she said. "There's a roadblock a little further north. The policeman said something about an airfield."

"Nothing to worry about. They don't patrol in the rain. And the lorry is empty. We have nothing to hide."

He drove slowly, slogging along the muddy way until they reached a paved road on the outskirts of Tangier.

"An airfield?" he asked.

"That's what I think he said."

The downpour sprayed against the side of the truck and the tires hissed as they cut a swathe through the rain-heavy streets.

"One more thing to worry about," Adam said. "Eisenhower's been able to convince the French general in Algiers not to hinder the landings. But things are different in Morocco. The French chief of staff in Casablanca is afraid of Vichy, wants to make a show of resistance."

"Damn it. You make it sound like it's some kind of game."

"I wish," Adam said. "I wish."

In Tangier, the streets were like rivers in the afternoon dark, with no pedestrians and few cars, the wind bending the palm trees, fat raindrops hitting the surface of the water and making circles in the reflection of the streetlights.

Adam parked the pickup around the corner from the hotel. They ran for the El Minzah through the torrent, sloshing through water coursing over their ankles.

They trudged into the lobby, shaking off the rain, in time to see Korian slinking down the stairs into the lobby, his heavy liquid eyes drooping, giving his face a permanent façade of weariness or guilt.

Lily could never tell which.

He seemed startled when he saw Lily. "I come here every Tuesday for tea and bridge."

"No need to explain."

He had covered the hole in his lapel with a small pink rosebud. "It's a bridge club. The British Whist Association."

"Whist?" There was a different smell to him today.

"That's what they call it. You can ask upstairs."

"I believe you." Cigars. That's what it was. "You've been smoking a cigar?"

"I always do at the Tuesday Whist. Can't smoke them in the Legation." By now, Korian had maneuvered to the door. "Have to run. My taxi is here."

He hurried into the street.

They watched him leave and started up the stairs.

"All I want is a hot bath and some dry clothes," Adam said. "I'll call you in an hour. If you're up to it, we can talk over dinner."

As they reached the hall, Lily thought she saw a billow of orange pantaloons disappear around a corner.

She found her key and opened the door.

Inside the room, Drury sat in the chair facing her, his face purplish and swollen, jaw slack, blind eyes bloodshot.

Lily backed into the hall, colliding with Adam, feeling panic mount in her throat.

Adam caught her by the shoulders, stifled her scream with his hand over her mouth. "My God! He's dead."

He led her into the room and shut the door. "I have to get the code box from Drury's room before we call the police. Be right back." His face was bloodless with shock, and his hand quivered as he stroked her cheek and traced under her chin. "You'll be all right?"

She was too numb to answer.

He reached for her shoulder and his arm fell to his side. "May as well change out of those wet clothes. You'll catch your d.... Oh God damn!" He stood at the door, twisting the knob. "Be back soon."

The lock clicked when he shut the door behind him.

Lily averted her eyes, trying not to look at Drury, and reached into the closet.

Keep moving.

She clung to the edge of the room as she made her way to the dresser.

She fumbled open the middle drawer and reached inside for underwear, feeling the clothing damp against her neck and stretching across her back. She was trembling now, scarcely able to move.

On her way to the bathroom, she passed Drury and her eyes turned away.

She sidestepped into the bathroom and shut the door. Hardened pieces of the mashed potatoes Drury had packed around the microphone were strewn on the floor like bits of yellowed plaster. The grid from the airway lay across the sink, leaving a residue of soot when she moved it away to turn on the water.

The walls of the bathroom swirled around her and she clung to the sink for balance, overwhelmed with a feeling of unreality, floating in a dark void, soul-scarred and empty.

She rubbed her wet head with a towel, pressing harder and harder, faster and faster, until the muscles in her neck ached. She changed out of her wet clothes and, still shivering, opened the bathroom door. Back into the bedroom, back to where Drury sat in the chair, the lamplight glaring on his mottled face and lolling tongue. A microphone lay on the table next to his clutched hand and a wire was tight around his neck.

This time, she screamed and couldn't stop.

Chapter Twenty

Footsteps pounded through the hall, strangers pressed into the room—the desk clerk with a frightened face, Adam Pardo shaking his head no. No code box, no Rafi, no Drury, no screaming.

Two policemen from the Guardia Civil came through the door. One of them, a lieutenant, advanced toward her speaking, his mouth moving, his arm gesturing.

"Miss Sampson," he said again in English. "Miss Sampson. You will come with me."

Lily sat on a low stool in a room with a high window, her wrists handcuffed to the legs of the chair, her shoulders hunched over, a policeman on either side of her. A pair of floodlights blazed into her eyes.

She had been here all night, in spite of protestations that she worked at the Legation, in spite of her request for diplomatic immunity.

"You don't have a diplomatic passport," Lieutenant Periera insisted.

"Call the Legation, they'll tell you. Speak to the chargé d'affaires, Artemis Boyle."

"The Guardia Civil office is closed. We can't make the call until tomorrow morning."

She had almost asked to speak to Major Pardo, then thought better of it.

"No one called about me?"

"Should they have, Miss Sampson? You have an arrangement, a code, a signal?"

I'm on my own.

"You were in your room with Drury for ten minutes before your screams were heard," the lieutenant repeated. He stood on a platform that ran around the edge of the room, gazing down at her with steely resolve. "What did you do in those ten minutes?"

Cold and exhausted, she closed her eyes. The lights burned through her eyelids with a red haze. Drury's face in the light of the lamp, blotched and swollen, loomed before her.

"You didn't get along with Drury," a voice said. "You argued with him. No secrets in Tangier, Miss Sampson. You fought with him in public two days ago." The voice was clipped and hard. "A lover's quarrel?"

The room buzzed around her. Her head sank. Drury's face wouldn't go away. Will I always remember him like this? Will I forget the tall, gaunt man with the thatch of white hair and the quizzical eyes?

"Open your eyes," the voice demanded.

She felt herself pitching off the chair.

"Your door was locked. I repeat—"

She thought of Rafi, and remembered him smiling. Rafi who defied the Panzer Division. Where was Rafi now?

"Look at me, Miss Sampson," the voice said.

Someone grabbed her hair and yanked back her head, arching her neck, pulling her backward until she felt the pressure on her manacled wrists.

The lieutenant loomed over her. Beyond the glare of the floodlights, the pearly white sky of morning glimmered through the patch of window.

"You had an accomplice, Miss Sampson. You couldn't have killed him by yourself. Who was your accomplice? Major Pardo? Your other lover?"

"I told you, I didn't...."

"Whoever it was, we'll find him, Miss Sampson. There are remnants of skin and blood under Drury's fingernails. The man who helped you has scratches on his hands and arms."

Periera waited for an answer.

"I can understand, Miss Sampson," he said, softly this time.

He paused, shot a glance at the policeman by her side, nodded and stepped down to the floor of the room. The policeman released Lily's hair and her head fell forward.

The lieutenant leaned toward her. "I can guess what happened."

His tone changed. He spoke into her ear, almost whispering, as if he were confiding in her. "You are an attractive woman, Miss Sampson. Drury lurked in your room, made advances, pressed you. Isn't that so?"

Lily didn't answer.

"And someone came to your rescue," he continued in an unctuous voice.

"I need to sleep."

She closed her eyes again. This time she saw Rafi, caught in the crossfire, blown up in the minefield.

"You don't have to hide the identity of your defender, Miss Sampson," the voice said. "He protected your honor. I would have done the same."

She looked up at Periera. "I didn't. No one—"

The door behind the lieutenant opened. Another guard came into the room. The lieutenant rose, conferred with the guard and they left together.

Lily closed her eyes and slumped on the stool. She felt herself falling into a red cloud. The pressure on her wrists pulled her back. She wrenched awake, looked around the room, closed her eyes again.

She heard a door open, heard footsteps, heard the lieutenant's voice drone at her.

He barked orders in rapid Spanish.

Someone unlocked the handcuffs, pulled Lily from the stool, led her onto the platform and out of the room.

"The American chargé d'affaires pretends that you work at the Legation," the lieutenant said as they moved her down the hall. He marched ahead, his heels clacking along the corridor. "Claims you have diplomatic immunity."

In the lieutenant's office, Boyle sat in a slatted wooden chair that faced the desk. A policeman stood Lily next to Boyle and left the room.

At the desk, the lieutenant moved his chair, smoothed his sleeves, and straightened the blotter and tray on his desk. "And what do you do at the Legation, Miss Sampson?"

"I already told you," Boyle said. "She's the cultural attachée."

The lieutenant reached for a paper clip in the tray. "And what do you do as cultural attachée?"

"She maintains contacts with locals," Boyle said quickly. "Gives out information about American culture, informs our personnel about customs and beliefs of the native population."

"I was asking Miss Sampson. She can speak for herself." He stopped, looked down at his hands and played with the paper clip. He twisted the wire into an S, kept twisting until it snapped in two. "What are your duties, Miss Sampson?"

Only two chairs in the room. Lily could feel herself swaying.

"I'm waiting, Miss Sampson."

Boyle stood up and motioned Lily to the chair.

She sat. He's waiting for an answer. "I...." What did I do at the Legation? "A... a handbook on Rif culture for our staff."

A piece of the broken paper clip scudded to the floor when the lieutenant threw it down. "How long has she worked for the Legation, Mr. Boyle? Since yesterday? Last week?"

"Since she arrived in Tangier to do archaeological research under the auspices of the State Department."

Periera grasped a worn green passport embossed with a gold American eagle, picked it up and waved it in the air. "I have her passport here." He slapped it on the desk. "I repeat, Miss Sampson, it is *not* a diplomat's pass."

Boyle took a step toward him. "You doubt my word, Periera?" His indignation rang in the room, too broad, too pat. "Colonel

Yuste will hear of this. Insulting American representatives, abusing members of our diplomatic corps."

"Colonel Yuste will indeed hear. An American national was killed and the chargé d'affaires offers a lame excuse to demand release of our principal suspect." Periera paused, letting a hint of warning hang in the silence. "Diplomatic immunity indeed."

Periera picked up the passport and leafed through it. "Interesting document. Palestine, England, Egypt. You are well traveled, Miss Sampson. What is it you do exactly?"

"I dig. I'm an archaeologist, an anthropologist. I excavated in the caves on Cape Spartel until–-"

Periera opened the passport to the first page. "The picture hardly does you justice."

He tossed it back on the desk and turned to Boyle. He waited. Lily closed her eyes and heard Periera's voice again.

"Miss Sampson? Miss Sampson, did you hear what I said?"

Lily opened her eyes, too frightened to speak, too tired to care.

"Did you hear me, Miss Sampson? You may leave for the time being. Return to what Boyle calls your official responsibilities."

Outside, Boyle guided Lily toward an old Packard parked at the curb. A small American flag fluttered from a stick perched on the right fender.

The glare of the overcast morning burned Lily's eyes.

"I can't go back to that hotel room," she told Boyle. "Not after—"

"Major Pardo took care of it. Brought your things to the Legation, set them up in the room next to your office."

Lily shuffled along the sidewalk toward the Packard.

"You look terrible." Boyle reached into his pocket and handed her a comb. "At least, try to comb your hair."

The comb slipped through Lily's fingers. "I'll be staying at the Legation?"

Boyle opened the passenger door for Lily. "You have your own bathroom down the hall." He picked up the comb from the sidewalk. "Tiled. Very Moorish."

He got behind the wheel, started the engine and turned to her. "Pardo filled me in on what's happening and your role in it."

"Oh? What role?"

"Torch." He sounded annoyed. "Everyone seemed to know but me." He pulled away from the curb. "I don't appreciate being kept in the dark."

"No one meant to insult you."

He maneuvered the portly car through the narrow streets of the medina, sounding the horn, scattering the carts, donkeys and foot traffic that clogged their path.

"I could have helped, you know," she heard Boyle say, his voice coming from far away.

She was already asleep.

Chapter Twenty-One

Lily fell onto the bed without washing her face or changing her clothes, the squeaking bedsprings sinking under her weight, the straw mattress rattling like paper. When she awoke, a down comforter covered her, a pillow was under her head, and it was night. Five red roses were arranged in a tall glass on the table next to the bed.

She closed her eyes again. After a restless sleep of disordered, unremembered dreams with heart-pounding fear, she awoke, still grinding her teeth in futile anger.

The corridor was empty. Only night sounds ticked in the still hall. She made her way down to the bathroom and washed, wrapped herself in towels and padded back to the little room with the bed, feeling the cold floor of the corridor beneath her feet. She found a nightgown in the chest of drawers and crawled back between the quilts.

She sank into a fitful sleep of gore-soaked images—arms and legs exploding in death; bloodied purple faces; muffled screams; Rafi and Drury calling out in agony. She awoke exhausted, her head wracked, her eyes grainy and burning, as if she had sobbed all night.

She soaked in a steaming blue tile tub in the bathroom down the hall, finding a jar of bubble bath and a bar of perfumed soap, still in its wrapping, on the edge of the tub.

Dizzy from the hot water and the pattern of the tiles that surrounded her, she dried herself and felt the hamsa, cold and wet against her skin. She had forgotten it and fingered the chain, still around her neck.

Keep me safe, indeed.

Consumed with a pervasive sadness, she dressed and went out into the cold dawn. She wandered through the quiet streets and found herself on the beach, listening to the slap-slap of eternal waves. She took off her shoes and walked along the strand, feeling the sand cool and sharp between her toes.

She brushed the sand off her feet, slipped on her shoes and strolled aimlessly toward town through a patch of weeds cluttered with broken glass and shreds of half-rotted paper that shivered in the wind, nettles scraping against her shins.

Across the way, she saw a low wall surrounding an incongruous English garden——roses choked with leggy flowers and the cloying smell of jasmine. She turned away.

"I'm sorry, dear child," she heard a voice call after her, almost the sound of a whisper. "So sorry."

Lily turned back to see MacAlistair's aunt, Emily Keane, leaning on the arm of her grandson Phillipe near the garden wall. Lalla Emily gestured with her cane for Lily to come closer.

"My morning constitutional," Lalla Emily said. "These days, I go no farther than my garden wall."

Lalla Emily's gaze seemed to penetrate into Lily's soul. "You're mourning someone deeply. I see it in your face. You were that fond of Dr. Drury?"

"It isn't only Drury." Lily felt hollow inside.

"Someone you loved? The wound seems to be beyond words."

Lily's eyes clouded with tears and they coursed down her cheeks. She wiped them away with the back of her hand.

"He was killed in the war?" Lalla Emily asked.

Lily nodded.

"When sorrow is still fresh, the pain is raw." Lalla Emily put her weight on her cane and moved closer to Lily. "But you'll get through it, you'll come out changed on the other side and nothing will be the same."

"I don't want to change."

I want it all to go back the way it was. Last week, last month, last year.

Sobs choked her and the tears kept coming, streaming down Lily's face and trembling on her chin. Her nose began to run. Phillipe held out a handkerchief.

"You weep only for yourself." Lalla Emily paused. "Sighs and tears change nothing."

"I weep for Rafi."

"That was his name, Rafi?"

"I want to talk to him, to see him, to hold him."

"You can't bring back what is gone."

Lily shook her head.

"You'll get past this." Lalla Emily's voice was scarcely more than a threadlike breath. "But the sadness will always be with you." She steadied herself. "Yours is not the first tragedy in the world. Your friend was not the only soldier." She reached out and put her free hand on Lily's arm. "I'm not cruel, my child. Just remembering. And experienced in death."

Lily handed back the handkerchief. Phillipe folded it into his pocket, his eyes warm with sympathy.

Lalla Emily took Phillipe's arm. "I tire easily these days. I must take my leave." She turned slowly. "Please, my dear," she said to Phillipe. "Let us go inside."

◇◇◇

Back at the Legation, Adam paced the hall outside of Lily's room.

"You all right?" He examined Lily intently and chewed on his lower lip. "We have a lot to do. Less than forty eight hours to Torch."

Still dazed, Lily looked at him.

"Torch," he repeated. "The landings at Casablanca. Lives depend on us."

Other lives. Other battles. Other soldiers. "I can't."

She ran into the bedroom, slammed the door behind her and slumped onto the bed, eyes hot with tears.

She burrowed into the covers, sobbing, desperate, faint with images of a phalanx of soldiers, faceless under steel helmets, bayonets fixed before them like the quills of porcupines, advancing in terror into an abyss. One had Rafi's eyes.

"I can't, I can't," she said aloud.

Without thinking, she reached for the hamsa again. She remembered the last letter she received from Rafi, remembered he had written, "I would do anything to stop them. Anything."

There was a gentle knock on the door. Adam's voice called out, "Lily?"

"Beat them back into oblivion," Rafi had written.

The sadness will always be with you, Lalla Emily had said.

"You all right?" Adam's voice said.

She stood, wiped her eyes and straightened the folds of her skirt. She opened the door.

"Not all right. But ready as I'll ever be."

She sighed and followed him down the hall.

Lily and Adam sat at a table in the Petit Socco nestled in the shadow of the Great Mosque with its green and white minaret, oblivious of the hubbub crowding past the little café, of the hawkers, the prostitutes prowling for clients, the shoeshine boys, the dark-veiled housewives heavy with packages. The muezzin had just called the mid-morning prayer. They ate a breakfast of rolls and cheese and café au lait.

The woman with the poodle sat in the back of the café, rhythmically stroking her dog between the ears. She spoke to a man who hovered over her, his back to them.

"You see that woman in the far corner?" Lily said. "I saw her in the Wine Bar at El Minzah once, talking to the German who followed me."

"The woman with the dog? What's she up to?"

The man handed the woman an envelope. She had a packet in her hand, slid it into his pocket, and withdrew her hand with an open palm.

"Who's that with her?" Adam asked.

The woman resumed petting her dog. The man straightened up, glanced over the tables in the café and hurried away.

Lily caught only a glimpse, but it was enough. "It's Korian!"

"Well I'll be damned." Adam put down his cup. "Needs looking into."

A woman in a dark suit and a lace blouse came up to their table and reached for the extra chair. "You mind if I take this," she said, smiling.

"We're expecting someone," Adam told her and the woman walked away.

Lily picked up another roll and buttered it, pondering Drury's death, wondering about Korian. "You think he has something to do with what happened to Drury?"

"Anything's possible."

"He can't be trusted," she said, thinking of Drury's comments about the bulletin. She told Adam about it, and about their fight.

"They didn't get along from the beginning," she said. "And we saw him at the El Minzah that day, when we got back from Asilah." Adam took another sip of coffee. "He said he was playing whist."

Adam glanced over at the woman with the dog. "Could be that the murder is connected to the Germans who stalked you."

"Drury thought they were working alone." Lily dipped her knife into the marmalade and spread it slowly on the roll. "You think he was wrong?"

"The Germans who were following you could have killed him."

"I don't think so." Her fingers were sticky with marmalade. "Zaid and Drury took care of them. At least, that's what I thought they were doing. That night, before we went to Gibraltar." She wiped her hands on a thin paper napkin beside her plate. "Almost the last time I saw Drury, except for…." Her voice trailed off as she remembered surprising him in the office with Suzannah. "You think Suzannah had something to do with it?"

Adam shook his head. "No. Someone who worked with the Germans, maybe. The wire and the microphone signaled—"

Lily turned to him. "Revenge? For what? For killing the German spies?"

"More than that. It was a personal signal. To you. You're in danger."

She thought about that, still numb with the events of the last few days, and rubbed her forehead. "It hardly matters."

"Of course it matters."

"I may be next?"

Adam nodded. "Sorry I dragged you into this mess."

He leaned forward, weary-eyed, his hand reaching for her arm.

"You didn't do it." Why didn't she feel more frightened?

"Your ordeal with the police was because of the delay in reporting the murder."

"You had to find the code box. It wasn't your fault."

Still, the memory of the stern face of Lieutenant Periera haunted her.

Lily shuddered. "Anyway, it's over."

"Not over yet. I have to leave for Casablanca tonight. Have to be there first thing in the morning. You'll be all right?"

She picked up the napkin and dabbed at her fingers again. "You found the code box?"

Adam shook his head no and scanned the teeming square. Korian's friend with the dog was still there and the woman who had asked for the chair sat at a crowded table, happily chatting.

"Later," Adam said.

A small man in a windbreaker and army pinks approached their table and sat in the empty chair next to Lily. It was Donovan.

"They told me I could find you here," Donovan said.

He looked around the café. A boy, no more than eight years old, was going from table to table, his face a mask of sadness, his hand outstretched to beg.

"Walk with me along the Strand," Donovan said to Lily.

Adam took a sip of coffee and sat back in his chair. "I'll wait here until you're finished." He glanced toward the woman with the poodle. "Watch the passing scene. If I'm not here, I'll meet you at the Legation."

Lily and Donovan started along the beach walk, past old colonial houses, past strollers out for the morning sun, toward the sea.

The shore was deserted except for a cluster of young boys about a hundred yards down the beach playing near the edge of the surf, running barefoot along the sand, their open shirts flapping in the breeze.

Lily and Donovan walked down to the apron of wet sand at the edge of the water.

"Drury filled you in about Operation Torch?" Donovan asked.

Lily nodded.

"His job was essential. The ships are lying off Casablanca on the Atlantic side right now, ready for the signal. We're using short-wave signals with a limited range, so messages have to be relayed from Allied headquarters in Gibraltar through Tangier before they're sent on to Casablanca." A cool wind off the ocean ruffled Donovan's hair. "We were counting on Drury to relay the messages in Tangier between Allied headquarters and Casa. You'll have to take his place."

"I know how to work the transmitter."

Donovan nodded. "Good."

At the other end of the beach, the boys chased toward the edge of the water as the waves went out, then ran up the sand, laughing, trying to beat the oncoming surf.

"The messages between here and Casablanca are encrypted. We're letting a few between here and Gib open. The Krauts and Vichy French suspect something. We want them to think the landing will be inside the Straits on the Mediterranean side, where their U-boats are patrolling." He paused and looked at Lily intently. "You know how to work the code?"

A wave moved up the beach and receded. Black and white oystercatchers stepped carefully along the edge of the water with their long legs in an endless dance, using their beaks to pluck worms and mollusks from the tiny breathing holes that popped out in the glistening sand.

"There's a problem," Lily told him. "The code box is missing."

"Missing?"

"We looked in Drury's room. It was supposed to be in the bureau, but it wasn't there. It's possible that whoever killed Drury has the code box."

"That puts the whole damned operation in jeopardy." Donovan raked his bottom lip with his teeth. "We don't have time to set up a new code. You have to find it."

"Even if we find it, suppose they broke the code."

"We have to take that chance. Find the code box."

Squeals came from the boys down the beach when the surf caught up with them, fanning high against their legs, dousing their clothes. A fresh November breeze blew off the water and Lily crossed her arms across her chest against the chill.

"You'll find it." Donovan smiled and gave her a thumbs-up. "After all, you have part of today and all day tomorrow."

Lily left the beach and made her way back to the little café in the Petit Socco.

Adam was not at the table. The woman with the poodle was gone, as was the woman who tried to borrow the chair.

Lily looked around for Adam and noticed a man near the entrance. He stood behind a large flowerpot planted with blooming oleanders. He had dark sandy colored hair, a trim beard and wore a striped kaftan and knitted skullcap. A Berber, perhaps?

Lily watched him. Something was wrong with the way he looked, something out of place. He moved slightly and she noticed his shoes—wing-tipped brogues. She could make out brown trousers with tailored cuffs showing under the hem of the kaftan.

She left the café, and the man with the wing-tipped shoes followed. She crossed the crowded Grand Socco, glancing back now and then. He was still behind her. She turned toward the Ville Nouvelle and took a fleeting look back. Still there. She hurried through the Place de France onto Boulevard Pasteur. The man with the wing-tipped shoes kept pace with her at a discreet distance, from the other side of the street.

She turned down the Rue de France, slowed down to a leisurely stroll, halting now and then at shop windows. He was still with her, still on the other side of the street, stopping when she stopped, moving when she moved.

She paused at a shop that displayed sweaters and skeins of wool, and watched the other side of the street through the reflection in the window.

The man was gone. She began walking again, and then she saw him, saw the sandy beard and the wing-tipped shoes. The kaftan and the skullcap were gone. He wore a tweed sport jacket now over his brown slacks and carried a bulky shopping bag.

She turned a corner into a side street and checked the other side of the road. He followed. She turned, reversed directions. He did the same.

She halted. The man stopped near a kiosk, stared down at the newspapers and fingered his beard, then disappeared into one of the shops.

He was gone. But the man with the icy eyes, Gergo Ferencz—the Hungarian who ran German intelligence in Tangier—stood in front of her.

Chapter Twenty-Two

Ferencz moved toward her, swiftly and smoothly as a snake. He grabbed her arm and twisted it behind her and levered it upward. The pain reached up her arm into her shoulder.

"The landing," he said and jerked her arm. "When and where?"

The pain was more intense now, reaching across her back. She flailed at him with her free arm and tried to kick him.

Few people were in the street, a workman carrying a box on his shoulder, a woman coming out of a bakery.

Ferencz pushed her elbow higher. "Where?"

He grabbed at her other arm. She struggled, stomped on his foot with her heel, and began to scream.

"Rape!" She struggled and screamed louder. "Rape."

The woman from the bakery stopped and then scurried around the corner. The workman dropped the box and began running in their direction. An Englishman in a dark suit, carrying a briefcase, came out of a doorway.

"I say!" He started toward them.

Ferencz loosened his grip.

She broke free and began running, turning the corner, sandals slapping the sidewalk, dodging pedestrians in the way. Ferencz ran after her.

She stumbled against tables strewn along the sidewalk outside of cafés, and tumbled over chairs that blocked the way.

Ferencz was gaining.

She collided with a woman, sent her hat flying, and kept running. She careened across the Place de France, onto the Rue de Statut.

Ferencz was still with her.

She ran up the street, through the café across the street from El Minzah, lungs burning, heart pumping.

She thought she saw Suzannah seated there, rising up to greet her. She darted across the street to El Minzah.

She glanced back from the door of the hotel and saw Suzannah and Ferencz, her arm linked in his, smiling at him, stroking his hair, murmuring in his ear.

Lily ducked into El Minzah, ran down the stairs, through the Wine Bar and out the side door.

No one was in the alley. She found a pile of clothes by the steps, ready to be picked up. She rummaged through the pile and found a heavy old brown coat that smelled of mildew, a hat no Berber woman in her right mind would wear, and a battered man's umbrella with some broken ribs.

She put on the hat, the coat, furled the umbrella, and tied it closed with a string she found around a bundle of clothes.

She hunched over in the coat to look smaller, and using the umbrella as a cane, began walking with a limp, dragging her foot behind her, through the empty alley to the fondouk market. She jostled her way through the market bent over in the bulky coat, still leaning on the umbrella, still dragging her foot, shambled down the stepped street and hobbled across the square, glancing behind from time to time to see if she was followed.

Just before she reached the steps that led to the Legation, she came face to face with Herr Balloon.

He blocked the way, glaring at her, hands at his side, flexing his fingers.

She stepped back.

He lunged at her, thumbs forward, tried to wrap his hands around her neck. The coat collar bulged around his fingers.

He cursed and tried again.

She ducked. The hat fell to the cobbles. She kicked it away and tried to ram him with her head.

His breath smelled of rotten teeth.

He stumbled and came at her again, this time grabbing for her arm and clutched only the bulk of the coat.

There was spittle on the side of his mouth.

She slid out of the sleeve and tried to stomp on his foot, kick at him. He swung at her with the back of his hand and she staggered back.

The coat dropped to the ground. He reached for her again. She tried to sidestep, lost her balance and leaned on the umbrella to steady herself. It bent, and she fell onto the coat, the umbrella clattering to the cobbles.

He raised his left leg, ready to stomp on her. She scrambled for the umbrella, caught the handle around his right ankle and tugged.

He staggered and she yanked again.

He fell backward. His head bounced on the pavement with a hollow sound.

She stood over him, dug the point of the umbrella into his side, and leaned into it.

He grimaced and stiffened, then his arms and legs flailed wildly with rhythmic, jerking movements.

She watched for a moment, frightened, then ran through the arch and into the alley that led to the Legation.

She waved at the Marine on duty at the entrance, and hurried inside.

Chapter Twenty-Three

Adam closed the double doors of Drury's office and turned to Lily.

"What happened to you?"

"We have to call an ambulance. We have to get a doctor."

"You're hurt?"

"No, no, it's not me. It's the German."

"What are you talking about?"

She told him about the man with the wing-tipped shoes, about the encounter with Ferencz, about the struggle with Herr Balloon, about his convulsions.

"Let it be," Adam said. "The German is an enemy casualty. Let them take care of their own."

"But still, he's hurt."

"He tried to strangle you, just as he strangled Drury."

"You think?"

"I think he killed Drury. He was working for Ferencz, he knew about the microphone in your room." Adam looked over at her. "I thought you said Zaid took care of the Germans."

"I must have misunderstood." She sat down at her desk. "I'm worried about what Suzannah is doing."

"What about Suzannah?"

"They know about the landing. They know about Torch. Suzannah is the leak."

"Suzannah? That couldn't be. Drury trusted her."

Lily told him about Suzannah's meeting with Ferencz, told Adam how Suzannah waited for Ferencz in the café across from El Minzah.

Adam listened. "This is bad." He ran his hands through his hair. "They know about the landing. They'll be monitoring all our signals. If they're not encrypted…." He sat down in Drury's chair. "We have to find the code book."

"And if they have it?"

"Then the whole damned operation is in the toilet. Another Tobruk. Could be a disaster. The whole offensive is at stake. Thousands of lives. If they break the code…." He sat at Drury's desk. His fingers drummed a nervous tattoo. "After the Germans broke the British code, Rommel overran the entire Eighth Army. A repeat of Tobruk, or worse."

"What can we do?"

"Not much. It wasn't in Drury's room. I searched it thoroughly."

"It might be somewhere in here," she said.

"Too late to change the code, too late to call off the operation. They're lying off the coast waiting for our signal, dammit."

The same thing that Donovan said.

"Even if they have the box, they don't know the code," she said.

"It won't take long to figure it out."

Lily watched the dust motes dancing in the stark morning light that streamed onto her battered desk. "Bureau?" Lily traced her finger along the surface of the desk. "Bureau is also an office, a desk. It must be somewhere in here. In Drury's desk."

Adam leaned forward in the chair. "You think?" He tugged at the drawer. "Locked. Maybe Boyle has a spare key."

Footsteps ticked along the tile of the hallway and stopped before the door of the office. Lily and Adam waited silently, listening for the steps to recede. Nothing.

Adam crept to the door, motioning to Lily to stand on the other side. She pressed her back against the wall.

He pulled at the door handle.

Korian stood with his hand poised to rap on the jamb. He composed a weak smile. "I came by to express my condolences." His mud-brown eyes oozed sympathy.

I'll bet you did, Lily thought.

"We saw you at the Petit Socco."

"You couldn't have." He didn't miss a beat. "I've been here all morning." His unctuous eyes arranged themselves into a sad expression as he clutched Lily's hand in both of his. "So sorry." He pumped her hand up and down. "You have my heartfelt commiseration."

Annoyed, she tried to pull out of his grasp and looked down. A gauze patch covered the back of Korian's hand. Lily recoiled, clasped her hands behind her back.

Periera's words—*We found blood and skin under Drury's fingernails*—rang in her head.

"Burned myself on the hotplate this morning," Korian said. "Nothing serious. And certainly not catching." He focused on Adam. "You're clearing out Drury's desk?"

"It's locked. Have to get the key from Boyle."

Korian reached into his pocket. "Use mine. These old desks all have simple locks. One key fits all." He turned to Lily, dangling the key in his hand. "Identical to yours."

Before he could advance on the desk, Lily intercepted him. She fished among the pencils and detritus of her top drawer, catching bits of broken rubber bands, smudging her hands on leaky pens, until she found the key at the back of the drawer. She pulled it out and swung it back and forth from ink-stained fingers.

"That's it," Korian said. "Same as every desk in the building."

He's waiting for us to open Drury's desk, Lily thought. She reached for his arm with her inky hand and stained his sleeve and the gauze patch on his hand. He grimaced and tried to rub the blotch with his fingers.

With her grubby hand still grasping his sleeve, Lily led him to the door.

"I'm sure you're busy." She gave him a farewell push. "We won't keep you."

She closed the door behind him and listened to his footsteps fade down the hall before she unlocked Drury's desk.

She pulled open the top drawer.

It was empty.

One by one, she unlocked the desk drawers and pulled them open.

All were empty.

Chapter Twenty-Four

She went down to Boyle's office and paused in the doorway, leaning against the jamb. Adam followed.

"Good news," Boyle said. "Rommel is in full retreat. Von Sturmer's been killed." He gave Lily a tentative smile. "You're looking better. Recovered from your ordeal?"

"Almost." Adam stood beside her. She could feel his body heat, his breath on her neck.

"If you're free," Boyle said to her, "come into my office and sit down." The smile was gone now. "We have to talk."

"Someone's been at Drury's desk," she said.

"I cleared it out. We packed his things to ship back to the States." Boyle stood up. His glance took in both Lily and Adam. "Either of you know any of his relatives?" Boyle asked. "He's married, I understand. You know how to get in touch with his wife?"

"That won't work. His wife is a patient in a mental hospital. I'm not sure she would understand."

"Anyone else we can get in touch with?"

"I think he has a sister in Wisconsin," Adam said. "Can't remember her married name off the top of my head. It's probably in his papers. Why don't I see if I can find her address?"

"I'll tell my secretary to get on it."

"I'll go through the papers myself. Your secretary has enough work to do," Adam said. "I'll get a dolly and move the boxes down to Lily's office. With her help, it won't take long."

"Lily and I have something to talk over while you're gone." Boyle signaled her to come in.

He motioned Lily to a chair. She sat facing him, watching him fiddle with his pens. He does that when something bothers him, she thought and waited.

"This news is not so good. I heard from Yuste."

"And?"

"Periera got to him first. You've been expelled. Yuste declared you persona non grata, gave you just seventy-two hours to leave the Zone."

"What about diplomatic immunity?"

"That's the point. You lose it the minute you leave the Zone. They could pick you up, put you in a Spanish jail."

"Why?"

"Periera insists you killed Drury."

"That's ridiculous."

"I told him that. Periera has some cock and bull story about a lover's quarrel between you and Drury. I told Yuste some damn Nazi killed Drury. He wouldn't listen, insisted on his own version. I argued him down to one more day, but you still have to leave."

I can't leave now, Lily thought. It's D-day minus two. "What about Torch?"

"Can't be helped."

Traffic in dispatches between here and Torch HQ in Gibraltar will be heavy, Lily thought, especially after the landing. Adam will have to find someone to take my place, show him what to do—someone with security clearance, maybe someone from HQ in Gibraltar.

"Three days?" Lily said. "I could take the ferry to Gibraltar."

Boyle picked up a pen, put it down. "The British suspended operation of the ferry to Gibraltar for the next week."

Torch again. "I can take one from Cuesta to Algeciras."

"You can't. Algeciras is in Spain. The minute you set foot on Spanish soil, you'll be arrested."

"The train to Algiers?"

"Same story. You'll be going through Spanish territory." Boyle paused, tapped the desk with his finger. "Your only hope is to go south into French Morocco, hope they don't pick up on the Spanish warrant." He stood up.

Lily turned to leave, then hesitated. "About Korian…."

"What about him? You mean the trouble Drury mentioned?"

"More than that. He's been checked? He has security clearance?"

"He's a career professional in the State Department. Passed the exams and went through minor questioning and background checks like the rest of us. We don't have proof for Drury's accusation against him. Why do you ask?"

"It's more than that."

"You're suspicious of him for other reasons?"

"I've seen him pass an envelope and receive something in exchange three times. Once, with the German who was following me, once with a man near the harbor, and this morning at the Petit Socco, a woman with a poodle. I saw her make a similar exchange once with the German at the Wine Bar at El Minzah."

"I'm aware of Korian's little habit," Boyle said.

"He denies that he was at the Petit Socco this morning. His actions could jeopardize everything. Shouldn't he be relieved of his duties, arrested for treason in wartime?"

"That's a little harsh. He's a career man. His little habit might make him open to blackmail, but that's the principal danger. I'm trying to arrange a transfer to a less sensitive area, the Congo maybe. Heroin is harder to come by there. He'll have to fall back on whiskey."

"Heroin?"

"I thought you knew." He sat at the desk and fiddled with the pens again. "You thought—" He raised his hand. "No, not Korian."

"Still," Lily said. "Heroin. Doesn't it bother you?"

"It's endemic in the area." He looked down. "Maybe it should bother me." He shrugged and looked up again, hollow-eyed. "Maybe I've been here too long too."

"What about the lady with the poodle?"

He held out his hands in a gesture of helplessness. "She's a fixture here. The Guardia Civil can keep track of her clientele. Besides, if they picked her up, she would be replaced by another dealer before they got her to the Mendoubia." He paused and looked over at Lily. "I'll see what I can do."

Back in her office, Adam was stacking boxes on Drury's empty desk, an empty dolly beside him.

"You think the code box is among Drury's things?" she asked him. "What's his sister's name?"

"Haven't the foggiest," Adam said. "I'm not sure he has one. It was an excuse to go through his papers."

A young man, face ruddy as a farm boy's, appeared in the doorway. His campaign hat tucked tight under his arm, he wore officer's pinks and an Eisenhower jacket. His uniform carried no insignia.

"This is Warrant Officer Blufield," Adam said to Lily. "He'll be working out of Casablanca."

The boy was round-cheeked and barely past acne. He transferred the cap to his left side before he turned and held out his hand.

"Pleased to meet you." He stood at attention, his hair falling over his forehead.

"Relax, won't you." Adam canted back the dolly with his foot. "Be right back. Have to get the rest of Drury's things from Boyle's office."

The boy watched him leave and fingered the cap under his arm.

"The Major tells me that you're at the University of Chicago," he said to Lily.

"I have an ABD. I haven't finished my dissertation yet. It's in archaeology. It'll be a while before I can work on it. I'm here for the duration."

"I mean…." He shuffled, moved forward and halted halfway to her desk. "You know what I mean."

"I was at the Oriental Institute. But I've been working in Morocco for the past year."

He waited an awkward moment for her to say more.

"I came here with Drury to work in the caves outside of town. But now—." She shrugged.

She didn't want to remember, to explain it all over again.

"I just graduated from the U of C," he said.

"What field?"

"Linguistics. Actually, a double major, linguistics and math. Makes me an expert in crypto-analysis. That's why I'm assigned to the CIC."

"You work on codes?"

"Yes. Well, not really. Just send messages. But I'd like to work at Bletchley Park."

"Benchly Park?"

"Bletchley, outside of London. Hush-hush operation. Scuttle-butt is that they worked out a German code called Enigma that encrypts signals automatically using a series of revolving drums. Cracked the ciphers. Now they can intercept messages from the German High Command, even from Hitler." He hesitated. "That's the rumor, anyway."

"And you'd like to know what Hitler's thinking?"

"It's not that. It's the way the thing works, using symbolic logic, Boolean algebra, decision theory. Meta-mathmatics they call it. It's not just Alice in Wonderland anymore."

"Alice in Wonderland?"

"Charles Dodgson was a mathematician, did some early work in symbolic logic. But he's more famous for the books he wrote as Lewis Carroll. They say that when he was presented to Queen Victoria, she asked for a copy of his next book, so he sent her a treatise on higher mathematics."

Blufield's eyes fixed on an unseen horizon, the brightness in his face focused on some distant dream. "What they're doing at Bletchley is a new way of thinking. Going to change the world."

"Wars do that," Lily said.

"Mister Blufield!" Adam's voice was stern. He stood at the door balancing a dolly stacked with boxes.

"I'd like to be in on that," Blufield said. "Work on that sort of thing after the war."

"Mister Blufield." Adam's tone was colder, more threatening. "You've heard the saying 'A slip of the lip can sink a ship'?"

"I was only repeating scuttlebutt." He ducked his head and gave Adam a tentative smile. "Besides, she has security clearance. She's one of us. Anyway, I was thinking about the future, when the war is over." He threw up his hands in a gesture of apology. His cap fell to the floor. "It won't happen again." He bent over to pick up the cap.

"Damn right it won't."

Blufield kept his eyes down, looked at his shoes, ran the toe of his right shoe along the back of his pant leg.

"I'd better get going to Casa," he said, his face flushed.

"Damn right you'd better."

Blufield stood at attention, saluted, and left the room. Adam maneuvered the dolly into the office and rested it against the wall.

"Weren't you a little harsh?" Lily asked. "He's just a kid, fresh out of school. He said he won't do it again."

"That's the point. They're all fresh out of school. And if there's a mistake on the beach at Casablanca, they won't have a second chance. They won't do *anything* again."

He hoisted one of the boxes onto Lily's desk. "Let's get to work."

Lily told Adam about Yuste's order while they sifted through Drury's papers.

She held a pad covered with Drury's familiar scribble. "I miss him. Even the gruff sound of his voice, making demands, barking orders."

"He had panache, mostly flamboyant." Adam opened another box and stacked the contents on Drury's desk. "In his own way, he was brave, and brilliant, a little quixotic." He looked over at Lily. "Where will you go?"

"Back to the States, maybe."

"You can't cross the North Atlantic. It's swarming with U-boats."

"Other people are crossing. A whole invasion force."

"That's different. They're soldiers."

"Soldiers. Expendable, isn't that what they call it?"

Expendable—like Rafi. She thought of him crossing the minefield, caught in the crossfire.

That last second, did he know?

"They're soldiers," Adam repeated.

"And I'm not? It's a case of women and children first? How chivalrous!"

"You could look at it that way. I like to think of it as an adaptive strategy necessary for the survival of the species."

"Always the anthropologist."

He flipped through the last folder on the desk. "Can't help it. I'm just a poor university professor." He put the stack back into the box and reached for another.

"Not anymore. You're an army officer."

"An army officer." He sat in Drury's chair, his arms limp at his sides. "On the eve of ordering a thousand young men to their death. Just kids." Adam's voice rang hollow from the depths of the chair. "They could be my students. And I'm about to send the message that could blast them all to hell."

He stood up and dumped the contents of a box onto Drury's desk. "Only two more boxes and we're done. Doesn't look like the code's here." He wiped his forehead and raised his hands in a gesture of helplessness. "You'll be leaving. Where do you intend to go?"

"Boyle suggested French Morocco."

"Straight into a war zone? Giraud intends to make a show of resistance. God knows how severe the fighting will be."

"I'll go south, stay away from the coast. I might do an archaeological survey." Lily rifled through the papers on the desk and returned them to the box. "There's a Roman site, Volubilis."

"Where would you stay?"

"Moulay Idriss. It's a little town near Volubilis named after the first sultan of Morocco. His tomb is there."

"I need you here." Adam slammed down the Manila envelope he held and leaned over Lily's desk. "I'll talk to Boyle, see if he can get Yuste to change his mind."

"Not likely. Boyle's already tried. You'll have to find a replacement for me."

She sorted through another stack of notes.

"I can't find a replacement that easily."

"No one's indispensable."

Adam put both hands on Lily's desk. "That's not it." A pink flush suffused his face and he lowered his head. "I could assign Blufield to take over some of your duties here. But I don't want you wandering through a war. I want to keep an eye on you. Two eyes, preferably."

Lily looked away. "I'll be all right. There's nothing to worry about. Nothing else I can do."

He went back to Drury's desk and began sorting through the rest of the papers. "I'll miss you." He opened a drawer and closed it again. "You'll need transportation. I'll talk to Boyle." He lifted a folder from the pile, thumbed through it, tossed it aside. "I may be able to arrange a jeep."

"I don't need—"

"Stay in the south 'til the beachheads are secured. Then you can come up to HQ in Casablanca. But not until the fighting is over." Adam stacked the folder he held on top of the others. "You can have my jeep. I'll requisition a command car to go to Casa."

He returned the stack of folders to the carton and held up an envelope. "There's a letter here. It's addressed to Suzannah. 'In case of my death,' it says. He was expecting something like this."

"Why Suzannah?"

"He trusted her more than you do." He put the letter in his pocket.

He reached the bottom of the carton and sank into Drury's chair. "That's the last of them. The code box isn't here."

"Maybe it's in the villa," Lily said. "If I'm going to do a survey, I'll need a theodolite. There's one at the villa, on the roof behind the radio, under the table where the boxes are."

"Theodolite?"

"It's like a transit, used in surveying. Measures horizontal and vertical angles, distances. I need it to map Volubilis."

"The code book could be in one of those boxes. We didn't look there yet."

"You think the code box is at the villa? Let's go up the Mountain and see."

They left the Legation and started toward the taxi stand in the street across from the steps. When they passed the steps, Lily stopped. The German was gone. The hat was gone, the coat, the umbrella.

Lily stared down at the cobbles where the German had fallen. "He didn't kill Drury."

"What makes you so sure?"

"If I could fight him off, so could Drury. Drury had special training for that." Adam looked over at her. "It was someone he knew. Someone he trusted."

"Someone who knew about the microphone," Lily said, and thought about Ferencz.

Chapter Twenty-Five

The villa churned with chaos. Overturned chairs spilled into the courtyard; tables lay on their backs, legs extended into the air; silk cushions, shredded and tossed, toppled across the floor. The garden tumbled with loose paper that swarmed before the wind.

The thuza wood vitrine was splintered, its glass doors shattered. Smashed artifacts and figurines lay scattered on the tiles and the head of the Berber from Volubilis was broken off the plinth.

Lily tripped over a broken jar that crunched beneath her shoe. "What's going on?"

Suzannah stood in the courtyard, her hand over her mouth. "MacAlistair is dead." Her hand dropped to her side. "I found him this morning."

"MacAlistair?"

Zaid scurried from room to room, gathering and redepositing bits of wreckage, cradling stacks of papers and old magazines to his chest.

"What happened?" Lily asked him. He gazed at Lily, swaying, his cheek covered with a plaster bandage. His eyes glinted with tears.

He dropped the papers that he held onto the floor and stepped over them. "He just floated off into the night."

"I summoned the doctor," Suzannah said in a dull voice.

Zaid picked up another chair and upended it. Had he gone mad? Creating the disorder, not clearing it up.

Lily stared at him, uncomprehending. "What are you doing?"

"Trying to make it look like forced entry into the house," Suzannah said in the same flat monotone. "A robbery, maybe."

"Why?"

"The doctor called police. He said MacAlistair was suffocated." She made a helpless gesture with her hands. "He said MacAlistair struggled. The pillow on his bed is streaked with the blood he coughed out."

"MacAlistair murdered? Why?" A flush of shock and vertigo roiled through Lily and she turned to Suzannah. "How do you know he struggled?"

"The doctor said."

"You called the police?" Adam asked.

"The doctor called." Suzannah indicated Zaid with a tilt of her head. "He's been acting like this ever since."

"The roof," Zaid said.

"The police? The Guardia Civil?" Adam started for the stairs. "Have to get the transmitter out of here before they arrive."

Zaid lifted a watercolor of a bucolic English scene from the Lake Country off the wall. "I'll keep them off the roof."

"Don't be too sure. Give me the keys to the Hillman."

"MacAlistair's favorite picture. He was brought up in a house near there, you know." Zaid dropped the watercolor onto the tile floor. "Have to make it look like someone broke in." The glass in the frame shattered and flew across his shoe.

"The keys," Adam repeated.

Zaid stirred at the broken glass with the toe of his shoe.

"Are you listening to me?" Adam advanced toward him. "Lives depend on it. We don't have much time." He held out his hand and cupped his fingers. "The keys!"

"On the hook by the front door."

Adam disappeared in the direction of the door and returned, keys in hand.

"Help me get the stuff together," he called to Lily. "Quick, before the police get here."

He vaulted up the stairs, two at a time.

Zaid began to sift the glass splinters through his fingers like a child playing in sand. "Nothing's right today." He fingered the plaster on his face and left a streak of blood from his fingers. "I cut myself shaving." He looked down at a bandage on his hand. "Broke the glass in the bathroom." He buried his head in his hands.

Adam's voice called from the stairwell. "Lily, are you coming?"

She found Adam in the far corner of the roof. He had already unplugged the equipment.

"The code box isn't here."

He pulled a travel case from under the table and opened it. "Without the code, the whole operation is in the toilet." He lowered the transmitter into the case and pulled out a smaller one to hold the Teletype. "We have to broadcast unencrypted." He looked at Lily. "You know what that means?"

"Maybe the Germans won't pick up the signal," Lily said. "You said that they use AM and we use FM."

"You think they don't know that?"

"Maybe they won't be able to respond in time."

"Maybe pigs can fly." Adam picked up a pad of paper and threw it down again.

Lily maneuvered out a wooden cube-shaped box with a handle that had been stashed behind the two cases. Beside it were a tripod and two stadia rods bundled together.

"Looks like the theodolite."

"See if the code book is in there."

Inside the box, she found only the surveying instrument, with its short telescope folded down. Extension wires, pencils, and pads of paper still lay on the table.

Adam began to wind one of the extension cords around his forearm. "I need another case."

"Maybe in MacAlistair's room," Lily said.

Adam tied the plug through the looped cord and picked up the next one.

Downstairs, Lily paused at the door of MacAlistair's bedroom, reluctant to enter, and drew in her breath.

I can't go in there.

Before she turned away, she saw a shadow float across the room. Lily moved inside silently, catching a glimpse of MacAlistair as she passed, his outline looming under a fresh sheet pulled over his face. Only the balding top of his head protruded, his scalp a purplish blue.

At the far end of the room, Faridah was opening drawers, pawing through the contents. Crumpled sheets lay in a bundle on the floor.

"What are you doing here?" Lily asked.

Faridah recoiled, her face colored. She lowered her eyes. "Zaid call me to help."

"I think he wants you to get the sheets out of here, take them downstairs and wash them."

"To wash the sheets?" She bent down to pick up the bundle and started out of the room while Lily rummaged through the floor of the wardrobe to find an overnight bag.

By the time she got back to the roof, Adam had already packed the transmitter and the Teletype. The only things left on the table were the rolled up extension cords and two pads of paper.

Adam jammed them in the overnight case.

"Faridah is here," Lily said.

"Who's Faridah? Tell me about it in the car. We have to get this stuff to the Legation."

He picked up both large cases by their handles and wedged the overnight bag under his arm and started down the stairs.

Lily followed, carrying the theodolite and the tripod and stadia rods under her arm, banging against the wall as she navigated the narrow stairs.

Adam called up to her, "What's keeping you? The car's loaded. Everything's in the trunk."

On the ground floor, Suzannah waited at the door. "It is possible I may ride with you? I must return to the mellah."

Adam grunted and Suzannah followed them to the car. Lily stashed the theodolite, the tripod, and the stadia rods on the back seat and Suzannah wedged herself into the back of the car beside them.

Adam started the Hillman, waiting a moment for the motor to warm up. "What the hell do you have back there?" he asked Lily.

"Digging equipment. Things I need for the survey."

"You've done surveys before?"

"When I first started graduate school. I got summer jobs on WPA projects in Texas and Kentucky."

Her mind was spinning with what she would have to do, what else she would need.

"Camera!" She opened the car door. "I need a camera."

"Later. We have to leave now."

"I don't want to come back when the police are here." Lily got out and slammed the door.

"Don't...." Adam said, but she had already started back to the house, running.

In MacAlistair's room, Faridah stood before the wardrobe, looking though the shelves. A camera was on the chair near the door.

Faridah held a book in her hand. *Rebecca.*

Lily dashed across the room, stopping next to Faridah. "I see you found my book."

She reached out and Faridah moved away. "Yours?" Faridah hugged the book to her chest. "Zaid say—"

"I looked everywhere. I forgot I lent it to MacAlistair." Lily searched in her pocket, found two pesetas and held them out to Faridah. "I'm grateful to you for finding it."

Faridah eyed the coins. Her grip on the book loosened. When Lily took it, Faridah shrugged, grabbed the coins, pocketed them and ran from the room.

Did Faridah know what it was? Lily weighed the book in her hands and fanned through the pages, dog-eared, with pencil notations in the margin. She closed the book, grabbed the camera, hurried to the car, and hurled herself into the passenger side of the front seat.

Adam was revving the motor, starting to back out of the drive, when a Volkswagen and a police car pulled up to the curb. "Damn! Now what."

A gray-haired man with a black doctor's bag got out of the Volkswagen and darted into the house as Periera emerged from the police car. With a ceremonious bow to Lily, he sauntered toward the Hillman. Lily stashed *Rebecca* behind her and leaned back in the seat.

Periera rested his arm on the open window on the driver's side and eyed Lily. "You claim diplomatic immunity again, I assume."

Lily felt the bulge of the book against her back. "Lieutenant Periera, how nice to see you." She forced a smile. "We're just arriving. Is something wrong?"

"Another murder. With you once more at the location of the crime."

"A murder? In the villa? Someone inside has been killed?" Lily widened her eyes in astonishment. "Who was it? When did it happen?"

"You claim not to know?" Periera asked. "As innocent as a kitten."

Adam released the brake. "I suppose we should leave. Won't keep you from your investigation," he said with a wave and put the Hillman in reverse.

Periera was forced to step back. He stopped, startled at the sight of Suzannah in the back seat. "You! Here?"

Adam rolled the car down the drive. Periera started after them as they gathered speed and the car hit the street. He followed them for a few steps, threw up his hands and set off for the house.

After they were on the road to town, Lily pulled out the book from behind her back.

"*Rebecca*?" Adam asked. "Where'd you get it?"

"Faridah was taking it from MacAlistair's room."

"I'll be damned. So tell me, who's Faridah?"

"She used to work at the villa. MacAlistair fired her."

"What was she doing there today?"

"Zaid called her to help out. But she was up to her old tricks, going through MacAlistair's things. It's a good thing I went back for the camera."

Adam looked over at her. "How are you going to carry all that stuff you have in the back seat? How will you handle a theodolite all by yourself?"

"I'll hire a Berber."

"You don't speak their language."

"I'll find one who speaks French."

"More likely, you'll find some drunken Frenchman who'll slobber all over you and offer to stay in your hotel room to protect you. I don't like it. I don't like it at all."

"I think your friend is jealous," Suzannah said from the back seat.

"I was going to ask you," Lily said, turning to face Suzannah, "how do you know Periera?"

"Ramon is a…." She hesitated. "A client." Suzannah looked down at her hands. She clasped them, fingers entwined, in her lap.

"And Ferencz," Lily said. "He's also a client?"

"Today was lucky. Usually I meet him in the evening."

"But today your appointment was for lunch."

"I had no appointment today. From Ramon, I tried to get information about the Spanish plans in Tangier, find out if they were preparing to join the Axis, let the Germans move south through Spain. From Ferencz, I tried to find out if the Germans were ready to move west through Tripoli or east to Egypt. Sometimes I was luckier than others, and I would pass the information on to Drury."

"To Drury?"

Suzannah nodded, still knitting her fingers. "I contacted clients that Drury was interested in. He told me what to ask, arranged somehow for me to meet them."

"Now that Periera saw you here—"

"I must flee again." She almost whispered, as if she were afraid of being overheard. "I can't go back to Marseilles."

"You're not from Tangier?"

"From France."

"Is that where you met Drury?" Lily asked.

"He knew my parents. They had a travel agency in Lyon. I was a secretary. When the Germans came, they took away my parents. I came home from work, everyone was gone, my daughter gone. The house ransacked. I ran away to Marseilles."

"Your daughter?"

Suzannah looked down at her hands again, clasped and unclasped them, her knuckles taut with tension. "Drury had come to the house and took our daughter before the Germans arrived. Some nuns came for her, hid her in a convent, changed her name."

"You said 'our daughter.' Drury is her father?"

"I don't know if I'll ever see her again. Only Drury knows where she is, and now…."

"You had a daughter with Drury?"

"We were close. Lovers. We knew each other a long time."

Suzannah rolled her bottom lip between her teeth again and again until it began to bleed. "Drury rescued me in Marseilles. I was arrested, some charge I didn't understand. It was too late to save my parents." She pushed back the hair that had fallen on her forehead. "He got me an American passport."

"You worked for Drury here?" Lily asked.

"I questioned clients who might have information for him."

"Didn't he object to the way you got the information?"

"At first. You have to understand. I will do anything—anything—to stop the Nazis." A tear started down her cheek and she wiped it away. "I ran from them once, and now I must run again."

"Where will you go?" Lily asked. "You have relatives?"

"Where?" Suzannah's voice trembled. "In France, all have been killed or taken by the Germans or fled, who knows where."

She lowered her head. Teardrops spilled on her clutched fingers.

After a while she said, "I may have distant cousins in Fez. I will go there."

She fell silent, her teeth still playing against her bottom lip.

Adam reached into his pocket. "I have a letter for you from Drury." He handed it back to her.

After a while, she said, "He tells me the name of the priest to contact after the war to find our child. God knows if the war will be over, if our daughter will survive, if the priest will still be alive. He says that he left us some money. There's no way to get it now, no way to get my daughter."

She didn't speak again until Adam parked the Hillman on the Rue de Portugal across from the Jewish cemetery.

She climbed out of the back seat, her eyes red and swollen. "Drury left a message for you. For both of you. If anything happened to him, he told me to tell you that the recipe for the blueberry pies is in the Bureau of the Djinn."

Chapter Twenty-Six

Lily watched Suzannah disappear into the mellah.

"What the hell is the Bureau of the Djinn?" Adam asked.

"The back of the cave where we dug."

"You know where it is?" Adam turned the key and started the motor, ready to go.

"Cape Spartel. The Caves of Hercules."

He revved the motor. "Let's go."

"We can't. The Spanish sealed off the area, put road blocks everywhere."

"There's no time to fiddle around. We have to get that code box."

"We can't get through. Maybe Tariq can do it," Lily said. "He knows the Bureau of the Djinn. Can you contact him?"

"No time for that. The Torch is lit tomorrow at midnight. We have to risk it."

"We'll go there tonight after dark."

He paused, sucking in his upper lip, working it with his teeth. "I have to be in Casa tonight."

"I'll go alone."

The car began to roll downhill. He put it in gear and turned the wheel to the curb. "Too chancy. You say the area's patrolled."

"I'll find someplace unguarded, maybe sneak through."

He turned off the engine and set the brake. "That's a big maybe."

"I can only give it a try."

He hesitated, his hand on the door handle. "Suppose you get caught. Then we've got nothing and Yuste will turn you over to the Nazis as a spy."

He got out of the car and opened the trunk. "I'll talk to Boyle, see if he can get you a diplomatic pass." He reached for the cases. "Have to get these instruments up and working before I leave."

He hoisted the small suitcase under his arm, picked up the boxes that held the transmitter and Teletype, and started toward the steps that led to the Legation. He paused at the arch. "You take care of the archaeological gear and lock the car. Bring the keys."

They stashed the equipment in her office at the Legation and Adam went down the hall to speak to Boyle. He returned, looking glum.

"He can't help. Says Yuste is inflexible. Boyle's tried to get permission before with no luck. Now, with you under suspicion, it's even harder." He picked up two cases. "Only locals are allowed in the area. They do I.D. spot checks. Even if you get through, you need papers."

He was already at the door, suitcases crammed under his arms. "I'm going up to the roof." From the hall, he called back over his shoulder, "Boyle wants to see you. He says it's about Meknes."

Lily stored the theololite and stadia rods in the little cupboard against the wall and started for Boyle's office.

Boyle told her Periera had called, insisting that Lily must leave in seventy-two hours. "Today's Friday. That means you must be ready to leave for the south by Monday."

Lily watched the nick in his nose quiver with each syllable as he spoke, giving his words an air of urgency. "Drury left cash with me in case of emergency. I guess this counts as one." He nodded his head as if going over it in his mind. "He left enough money for me to arrange transportation for you and room and board in Meknes. I'll get on it."

"I was thinking of staying in Moulay Idriss. It's closer."

"You can't stay there. It's a sacred site, the site of the tomb of the first sultan of Morocco and a close descendant of the

Prophet. Only Moslems are allowed to spend the night. You'll have to go to Meknes."

He stood up and came around the desk. "You sure you'll be all right?"

She turned to reassure him. "Of course I'll be all right."

She mounted the stairs to the roof and found Adam staring at a flagpole, the flag fluttering in the breeze off the sea.

"What's wrong?" she asked.

"Have to talk to Boyle. That flag means someone else has a key to this roof."

Lily looked around the roof paved with mosaic tiles, a low lip around the perimeter, and four outdoor lamp stanchions, all painted white. Large clay pots planted with leggy geraniums and marguerites stood at intervals along the edge of the roof.

"They use the roof for receptions sometimes," she said. "I was here last year for the one on the Fourth of July." She pointed to a shed in the far corner next to the flagpole. "The shed over there opens into a sort of buffet, where they keep the steam tables and barbecue. Electrical outlets are in the shed."

Adam fiddled with the keys in his hand, crossed to the shed and unlocked it. A radio–phonograph stood next to the bar on the left. Long folding tables and chairs stacked on their sides filled the right side. He opened one of the tables in the shelter of the shed, put the Teletype and radio on top and placed two of the chairs in front of the table. He plugged in the Teletype, motioned Lily to a chair, and pulled out a ladder from behind the stack of chairs.

Adam was on the ladder, attaching an aerial to the side of a storage shed when it began to rain again, at first just occasional drops. Sharp gusts slapped against the side of the shed. The flag snapped in the wind.

"Damn." Adam swayed on the ladder. "Wouldn't you know, the wind would come up when I'm in a hurry? Got to get this set up before dark."

The western half of the sky was rosy with sunset but to the east a starless sky, pearly with clouds, was already darkening.

Footsteps, indistinct at first, then louder, clattered on the stairway to the roof. A Marine from the entrance booth opened the door and another followed.

"Who the hell is that?" Adam asked.

The first Marine saluted. "Private First Class Jessup, sir." They moved toward the flagpole. "O'Hare and I came to take in the flag."

Adam gave a perfunctory salute. "You have a key to the roof?"

"I get it from Mr. Boyle, sir. In the morning to raise the flag and when we take it down in the evening before sundown."

They had already lowered the flag and begun to fold it when Adam came down from the ladder. "You finished, Jessup?"

"No sir." He held the flag taut as he stepped toward the other marine, turning the folds into triangles in a choreographed ritual. "We'll be gone in a minute, sir."

When they finished, they saluted Adam and disappeared through the door, locking it behind them.

"This place is busier than Grand Central Station," Adam said.

"For God's sake, they're on our side. It's no busier here than the villa."

"They don't have security clearance. Everyone in the villa had clearance. MacAlistair and Zaid are SIS."

"Which is?"

"Secret Intelligence Service."

"How about Faridah?" Lily asked. "Did she have security clearance too?"

"Faridah?"

In the lowering twilight, wind whipped against the panels of the shed, banging them back and forth. Lily grabbed the handle of one and held onto it.

"Faridah. The Berber woman at the villa."

"Never saw her before today. We won't go back to the villa." He climbed the ladder again. "I'll have the equipment up and running in a minute."

Lily stood in the shelter of the shed, out of the wind. Adam clambered down and turned on the transmitter. He adjusted the knob, typed out "Hello," tuned the receiver and loaded paper into the paten. After a few minutes, the Teletype clicked and printed "Hello back."

Adam let out a breath. "At least something works." He turned off the machine and looked up at the translucent, cloud-enshrouded sky. "They'll never make it. They can't land in this mess. Our first big offensive and the weather's against us."

He wrote some numbers on the pad next to the Teletype. "This is the frequency for Gib, this one's for Casa." He handed it to Lily. "Let's go downstairs. Figure out what to do."

He locked the shed and crossed to the door of the roof. "I'll send your replacement from Casa."

They stood on the steps below the closed door while he jiggled the keys.

He handed the key ring to Lily. "The round one's for the roof, the hexagonal one for the shed. Remember, round equals roof; hexagonal for six equals shed."

◇◇◇

Downstairs, Zaid sat in Lily's office, waiting behind Drury's desk, his chair canted back against the wall, his eyes closed, his feet up.

"How'd you get in here?" Adam asked.

"The door was open." Zaid righted the chair and put his feet under the desk.

"How did it go with Periera?"

"Fine. He's out looking for the two thugs who broke into the house and stole the Georgian tea service and the Delacroix and killed MacAlistair."

"MacAlistair didn't have a Georgian tea service, or a Delacroix," Lily said.

"Periera doesn't know that."

"Did they go up to the roof?" Adam asked.

"No. Too busy looking for what else might have been taken."

"You shouldn't be here," Adam said.

"I came to pick up the Hillman. I need to go to Medionna tonight."

"You can't get through," Lily said. "All the roads are closed. The area's heavily patrolled."

"I get through all the time. I know places the Guardia Civil never heard of."

"You're going to see Tariq?" Lily asked.

He shook his head and stood up. "No. The Mekraj. He's waiting for me in the village. I have a last message for him from MacAlistair."

"Could you make a stop on the way?" Adam asked. "At the Caves of Hercules?"

"Too much risk. There are gun emplacements on the headlands above the caves. The area's fortified. They shoot to kill."

"It's essential."

Lily interrupted. "I don't think he—"

"He'll make it. He can take you there." Adam turned back to Zaid. "Drury left something in the caves for her."

Zaid frowned. "What's so important about a piece of archaeological equipment?"

"That's not what she's after," Adam said.

"It's personal," Lily said. "There are things you didn't know about—about Drury and me."

Zaid raised his eyebrows. "Is it worth your life?"

Lily looked from Zaid to Adam, her head swirling with misgiving.

"Is it?" Adam asked her.

What was it Adam had said? With the landing, American forces were committed to their first big offensive. Rafi had walked across a minefield to stop the Germans in North Africa. She could do this.

"Yes." A sense of purpose tinged with apprehension eddied through her. "It's worth it."

"Then it's not archaeological equipment." Zaid ran his fingers across the top of his lip. "Or is it?" He paused, his forehead crumpled in thought. "I have to fix up papers, manufacture an I.D. for you." He narrowed his eyes. "Meet me after dark."

"At the villa?"

"No. The side street where I always park. Be there at eleven."

After Zaid was gone, Adam turned to Lily. "You know what you're getting yourself into? You're on your own."

"The code book is the key to the invasion. I can handle it."

"You'll have to. There's no turning back."

Chapter Twenty-Seven

Zaid waited in the Hillman, the motor running. Lily found a djelaba on the seat next to him. He was dressed as a Riffian in pantaloons and a vest, a white knitted cap on his head.

He picked up the garment from the seat and held it out to her. "Put this on and pull up the hood. If anyone stops us, I'll do the talking."

They took a southern route out of town, driving through areas unfamiliar to Lily, into the countryside, past hillocks and dark farmhouses. He turned onto an unpaved track with a drainage ditch running alongside.

A few feet past the turn, he stopped on the verge, next to the ditch. He reached under the seat for two license plates and took a screwdriver from the glove compartment.

"What are you doing?" Lily asked.

"We're in a different district. If we're spotted, they'll know we're from Tangier. Have to change the plates."

Lily waited in the car, looking around at the stillness, at the silhouette of a tree in the shadows, at hills in the distance, some with little specks of light. She listened to night creatures rustling through the leaves in the ditch and heard the soft hoots of owls, signaling location of prey.

She had never seen a night this dark.

Zaid got back into the car, tossed the screwdriver back into the glove box, and continued driving slowly along the rutted track.

"About Medionna," Lily said. "It's Friday. The Mekraj will be in Tangier for the Friday mosque."

"Oh?" Zaid glanced at her with a studied look. "It slipped my mind."

They drove in darkness, lights dimmed, the motor softly whining in low gear. Barely able to see ten feet in front of them, she watched the road, mesmerized by rocks along the side that cast long shadows, by small animals scuttling across their path, their eyes glinting in the murky gloom before they vanished into the fields beyond. Here and there, a light from one of the houses flickered in the darkness and disappeared.

"What was Faridah doing at the villa?" Lily asked.

"When?"

"Today."

"Helping. She can be trusted."

"I'm not so sure."

"She's my wife." Zaid hesitated. "In name only—a marriage of convenience." He had the flicker of a smile. "It gives me the right to beat her if she doesn't obey."

"Are you the one who forced her to work and didn't let her keep the money?"

"You remember that? This time she gets to keep whatever she wants." The smile became a satisfied smirk. "MacAlistair left everything to me."

"Is that why she was going through all his things?"

"My things."

Lily held her breath. "You killed MacAlistair."

"I promised him a long time ago. When things got bad with him, when he had nothing left but pain." Zaid hesitated. "I promised him, you know."

Lily sat rigid in her seat as they rode through the inky night in silence, wondering if she could trust Zaid, aware that it was too late, that she had no choice.

I must get the code book, relay the messages for the landings. At any cost.

Zaid turned the car into an open field and turned off the low beams. He leaned forward and squinted into the night, driving slowly across the field, the car pitching and straining as the wheels bit into the soft earth.

She saw only the sky, heavy with stars, through the mud-splattered windshield. After a while she could make out vague shapes in the darkness, a tree looming here, a boulder there. Wisps of fog moved past them as they approached the sea and soon they drove through a blanket of haze that wrapped them in a silent veil.

The air changed. Lily could smell the salt of the tide. Still surrounded by the cocoon of fog, the wheels of the car crunched over gravel, the sound almost drowned out by the crash and cadence of a furious surf.

Zaid turned the car beyond the gravel and parked so that it was pointed downhill. He turned off the motor, set the brake. "We're at the path below the caves."

He reached into the back seat for a pair of the headlamps they had used during the excavation and handed one to Lily. "Don't turn it on until we're inside."

They got out of the car, gently closed the doors and started up the path. They inched their way along the ledge toward the caves, clinging to the cliff face, hearing the angry sea pounding against the rocks below.

They moved carefully along the narrow shelf on stones slippery with night mist. Once, Lily lost her footing. Zaid reached out with his arm across her waist, holding her back until she steadied herself.

Her djelaba caught on a bush, the hood dropped down across her back. Zaid pulled it loose, tearing the cloth. He whispered a comment that was lost in the roar of the surf.

Finally, they reached the mouth of the Upper Cave.

Inside, Lily turned on the lamp and started toward the back of the cave, skirting the funnel that dropped into the lower cave.

She moved the headlamp up and down along the back wall, seeing nothing but the circular pockmarks that stonecutters had left behind when they pecked millstones and mortars out of the living rock. Instinctively, she reached for the hamsa hanging from the chain around her neck.

"Bismillah," she whispered into the hollow of the back of the cave and crawled closer to where the ceiling sloped down against the wall. Then she saw it—the glint of the metal latch of the code box wedged in a crevice where the ceiling met the back wall.

She tried to force it out, moving the box back and forth, her body taut with effort. Finally, she pried it loose, releasing the box with a shower of small pebbles and rocks. She toppled backward.

Before she regained her balance, she heard Zaid directly behind her.

"So that's what you're looking for. The code box."

Chapter Twenty-Eight

Lily steadied herself and turned around.

Zaid loomed inches away from her. "I've been looking for the code box. Drury said he hid it when I asked him where it was."

"He didn't tell you?"

"He said I didn't need to know. That was before—"

"Before he was killed?"

Zaid held out his hands in explanation. "He wouldn't tell me. What else could I do?"

Her spine prickled. The light from Lily's headlamp fell on his pantaloons. Bright orange. A shudder of fear ripped through her, remembering the flash of orange she had seen disappear down the corridor before she discovered Drury's body.

"You were in the hall that day. Running away."

"What hall?" His eyes narrowed, his jaw worked. "What day?"

"At the El Minzah. The day Drury was killed."

"Oh, yes. Had a feeling something was wrong." He came closer, leaning into her. "That's why I came to help you. I only had your safety in mind." He stopped, licked his lips, narrowed his eyes and looked off into the corner. "I wasn't there that afternoon. Must have been some other time." He reached out his hand. "The box is too heavy for you. Let me carry it."

She ducked and her lamp shone on the plaster stuck on his cheek.

"Cut myself shaving," Zaid had told her.

"Skin and blood under Drury's fingernails," Periera had said.

Zaid backed away, his face disappearing into the shadow. The light on his helmet trembled, swept the cave, focused on Lily.

"Hand over the box," he said.

She gripped it in her right hand. She could feel the book inside shift as she moved her left arm forward, hesitated, then swiftly pulled the plaster from his cheek and sprang back.

"What's the matter with you?" His fingers went to his cheek, hiding the cut.

But she had already seen the two deep scratches, like claw marks from a cornered animal.

"Cut yourself shaving?"

"Give me the book."

"Drury scratched you. Before you killed him."

"I told you. He wouldn't give me the book." He stood in front of her, his hand reaching out. "Neither would MacAlistair. Now you. You know what happened to them."

"You killed MacAlistair for the code book? He trusted you."

"Trusted me? He tolerated me. I was just part of his collection of exotica, a native, a colonial, to be condescended to, treated like a child. Drury too. All you Europeans are alike. You take up the white man's burden, tell us we don't know how to govern, set up protectorates for our own good, then rob us."

"We're Americans, not Europeans. We'll free Morocco."

"No you won't. You'll tell us we can't govern ourselves, like all the others. You don't understand. My ancestors ruled the civilized world while yours were still swinging from the trees."

He moved closer and she backed away.

"I spent part of my childhood in England, where they sent colonials like me to special schools where they taught us nothing and then said we couldn't learn. We had primitive minds, they said."

She tried to step around him but he blocked the way.

"Think, think," he said. "Where would your mathematics be, and your fine equations in physics if you had to calculate using Roman numerals, if you had no zero? Where did European science come from, with words like alcohol and chemistry and algebra? Before we taught you how to think like scientists, even your kings lived in unwashed ignorance and darkness."

He reached out and stroked her chin. "Be a good girl. I need the book."

She backed away. "It won't do you any good. You don't know the code."

He held out both hands now. "I already know it, pieced it together from decrypts scattered on the floor."

He's lying. Drury always cleared up, left nothing behind.

"Nothing to be afraid of." His breath came in short gasps, straining with controlled anger. "If you give me the book, I won't hurt you."

Lily stood perfectly still. The only other sound was the vibrating pulse of the rising tide slapping against rocks in the lower cave.

He came closer. "Give it to me."

She slid to the side when he grabbed for her arm.

The noise of the surf echoed through the chamber.

"Give me the book. Save yourself trouble."

He ran his finger down her throat. "How could I hurt you?" His finger traced her neck, gently circling the small depression where the hamsa rested, then up her throat again to her chin.

"The Hand of Fatimah." His fingers clasped the hamsa and pulled. "Supposed to keep away the evil eye. You believe it?"

Lily felt the chain tug against the back of her neck. "It was a gift."

"You're trembling."

She felt the pressure of his fingers on her neck, felt his breath against her cheek, the warmth of his lamp on her forehead.

A chill crept along her spine. The pressure increased.

Below them, the roiling sea was as loud as a train rushing through a tunnel.

She threw the box behind her on the floor of the cave. He dropped his hand and moved to pick it up. She kicked it away.

She drove her knee into his groin. He doubled over. She kicked at him, heard the thump as her foot connected with his shin.

He stepped backward to steady himself, his foot at the edge of the funnel. The ground collapsed beneath him. She watched him sink, stunned, into the hole toward the lower cave.

He gripped the side of the funnel. The soil crumbled under his fingers. He shouted.

"Get me out of here!"

She began to reach for him, sensed the ground soften beneath her feet, and jumped back.

"Help me." Zaid's voice was almost a whimper. "I can't swim."

She picked up the code box, giving the funnel a wide berth as she ran toward the entrance to the cave. Behind her, she heard Zaid's cry as he plummeted to the rocks below.

She closed her eyes and caught her breath. Don't look down, she told herself. But still, she imagined him splayed on the jagged rocks, his head split open, the pink froth of the surf foaming around him, the rising tide billowing against his legs.

From below, someone barked orders in Spanish. She turned off the light on the helmet and started down toward the Hillman.

Through the fog, she made out two soldiers from the Guardia Civil at the car. One had opened the door to look inside. The other inspected the license plate.

Flattening herself against the rock face, Lily moved down the slope. The shoulder of her djelaba caught on the roots of a tree growing out the of cliff face. She shrugged out of it and kept moving.

One of the soldiers looked up, pointed, said something to his companion. They started up the path toward the caves.

Lily hid in the crevasse of an outcrop.

The first guard lifted his rifle. *"Alto, alto,"* he called out.

She saw the flash of a gunshot trajectory, sniffed the acrid smell of cordite that drenched the mist. Behind her, the djelaba convulsed, seemed to dance in agony from the impact of the shot.

Running, the guards passed within a few feet of her in the fog, their footsteps crunching in the dirt.

Lily tried not to breathe.

They disappeared into the cave. Lily dashed for the car.

No keys. Zaid had the keys.

It couldn't be too difficult to start. Drury took less than a minute.

She slid to the floor under the steering wheel and turned on the beam from the helmet.

Multiple wires under the dash seemed to shift and coil like snakes with each motion of her head. She heard the soldier's voices again and footfalls along the path.

They're out of the cave. Coming toward me.

Which wire connects with what?

Steps sounded on the path, walking, then running, louder and louder, closer and closer. The guard's flashlight arced into the mist, shone and disappeared.

Lily turned off her light and scrunched lower. There must be another key. Maybe the glove compartment.

A light reflected against the back window. Lily groped for the glove compartment and fumbled inside. No key.

Nothing but the rusted screwdriver.

The explosive sound of gunfire smashed through the darkness. Bullets pinged against the rock wall, ricocheted against the car. It rocked. She covered her face with her arm. A shatter of broken glass spilled over her, stinging her hand.

In desperation, Lily grabbed the screwdriver, jammed it into the ignition, and turned it.

The motor started.

Chapter Twenty-Nine

Still scrunched below the seat, she twisted to reach the clutch. She put the car in gear and stretched to grip the choke.

The car inched down the slope.

Footfalls echoed behind her, pounding on gravel. Shouts of *"Alto, alto,"* bellowed in her wake.

She scrambled onto the seat, bent over, keeping her head low, below the dash. She grasped the door handle, cracked it open a few inches. Focusing on the ground, she rolled down the gravel path through the cloud of night.

A siren began to caterwaul. Behind her, a blur of headlights reflected in the fog.

She maneuvered the Hillman close to the cliff face and into a small indent. She waited, holding her breath, hiding in the dark vapors of the night, the cold and damp penetrating her bones, making herself small on the seat as if that would render her invisible.

If she turned off the motor, she couldn't start it again.

Let it idle. Maybe the shouts and sirens would drown it; maybe the crashing surf will mask the noise.

A patrol van sped past, sirens whining, multi-colored lights flashing through the whiteness of the night.

It worked. They didn't see the Hillman, didn't hear the motor.

They'll come back. What then? Think.

There's a turnout along here.

The reflection of red from the taillights of the patrol van receded.

So long ago since she had been here. Think. A few yards farther. Near where Suzannah's taxi had parked.

Slowly, carefully, Lily eased the Hillman forward and crept into the turnout.

She heard the whine of a motor pushing up the hill and ducked lower, huddled on the seat, hoping they wouldn't see. Her leg scraped against the glass shards on the floor and she jerked it back.

Approaching headlights whitened the night haze. The van passed and droned up to the headland.

In the reflected glare of their headlights, she saw blood caking over the slash on her hand, a new cut on her leg.

And then darkness.

She heard the thump of a slammed door cushioned by the fog, heard calls and shouts resound. She pulled herself up, glanced through the rear window. Halos of light moved in the blank whiteness that spread over the crest of the hill.

Could they see her through the curls of mist? She edged onto the road again, coasting into the white night. Could they hear the crunch of wheels on the gravel?

In front of her was nothing, the emptiness of haze. She was driving off the edge of the earth. She gripped the steering wheel and guided the Hillman, one hand on the partially opened door, watching the wheel of the car hug the edge of the macadam.

No one seemed to follow. She picked up speed, still watching the ground and kept going.

A car approached from the left, its lights shimmering through the foggy night. A crossroad?

She guided the Hillman to the side of the road. The headlights were closer, more intense.

Stay calm. Count to ten.

One. Two. Headlights brighter with each second. Still she waited. Five. Six. She listened for the oncoming car, steeled herself for the crash, arched her back, tensed her legs. Nine.

Ten. The light receded. No sound but the mournful blare of a distant foghorn.

Again the headlight reached out of the night and receded. Again the foghorn sounded, blanketed by the mist that surrounded her.

Lily let out her breath. Only the lighthouse on Cape Spartel.

She sat up, steered the car back to the center of the road, turned on her headlights, and peered into a wall of fog. She switched on the brights. The impenetrable whiteness of a netherworld loomed ahead.

She dimmed the lights and continued through the tunnel of fog, still monitoring her progress through the half-opened door, mesmerized by the whirl of tires along the macadam.

The whoosh of tires against the dampness of the road reminded her of the sound of the funnel collapsing, the floor of the cave crumbling away from her.

Zaid screaming, sliding down to the sea.

Again and again, against the blank whiteness, an image of Zaid splintered on the rocky outcrop at the bottom of the cliff haunted her.

Sacrificed to the gods of the sea.

Her teeth clenched, she shivered in the cold wind that blasted through the shattered windshield. Don't think of it. Have to get back to Tangier to light the Torch.

The fog lifted enough for her to close the door. She had almost reached The Mountain. She leaned forward against the steering wheel, moving cautiously through the darkness, peering at the road as it wound down the hill, feeling the damp wind sharp against her face.

Giddy with exhaustion, she began laughing at the image of driving through the Ville Nouvelle with a splintered windshield and a car raked with bullet holes, and couldn't stop.

What's wrong with me? I saw a man fall to his death and now I'm laughing.

Shaking.

Sobbing.

Take a deep breath.

What next?

Have to ditch the Hillman.

Where?

She had reached the villa. She parked the car in the drive and looked up at the bare windows.

Was Faridah sleeping in the quiet night, dreaming of her new luxuries, waiting for Zaid's return? Did she know he was sprawled on a bloody altar, an offering for someone else's safe passage through the Straits?

From the back seat, Lily retrieved the code box and started downhill toward the Legation on foot. She kept to the side of the road, clutching the heavy code box, the cut on her hand throbbing with the tightness of her grip.

Twice, cars going up The Mountain sped by her. She hid near the bushes and waited in the shadows. One car, full of revelers singing a sentimental German song, swerved toward her and away again, and she panicked, almost began running, until she caught herself and moved deeper into the brush.

Have to get back to the roof of the Legation, no matter what.

When the car passed, she moved out onto the side of the road again. She hugged the code box to her chest.

The turn of the war sits in the crook of your arm.

The fog dissipated. Lily had almost reached the Mendoubia when dawn broke, bright and clear, bathing the medina in a rosy glow.

Huddled over the code box as if carrying a stack of books to school, she found her way to the Legation.

Inside were quiet sounds, the creaking of old wood in the morning, stirrings in another part of the building. Sounds of wakening—water running through tired pipes, the smell of coffee.

Boyle.

She laid the code box on her dresser, locked the door with the old brass key, and went into the bathroom to wash.

She cleaned the cuts on her hand, laid a fold of gauze over them, and, awkwardly holding one end with her teeth, anchored the bandage with a plaster.

She thought of the poster in Drury's office in Chicago that she had seen so long ago, "What matters most is how you see yourself."

In the mirror above the sink she saw a tiger, tawny-haired and cat-eyed.

She turned off the tap and returned to the bedroom, still clutching the soiled towel. She dropped it on the bed, picked up the code box, and climbed the stairs to the roof. She opened the door and unlocked the shed. The flag was already raised, snapping in the wind, the metal hasps ringing as they struck the hollow pole. She sat at the table by the transmitter and lifted the heavy books out of the box.

Today was November 7. She turned to page 1107 in the *Bureau of American Ethnography Report XXXV*, reached for the graph paper and spelled out a message for Adam in code.

At eight a.m., she turned on the transmitter and sent the dispatch, "Have cookbook with recipes for blueberry pie. Can start baking."

A key fumbled in the lock on the door that led to the roof. The Marine?

Chapter Thirty

The door handle rattled, stopped, and started again. It couldn't be the Marine. Jessup was his name. The flag was already raised.

Lily rose from the table and closed the shed, heard the person jiggle the handle of the door to the roof, scratch at the lock.

Jessup had a key that worked.

The door banged and shook; the frame buckled.

She stepped back, listening, alarms clanging in her head.

The door exploded open.

Zaid stood on the landing, glowering at her, spewing hatred, eyes afire. Dried blood trailed down the side of his face from a gash on his forehead.

"The code book."

She took another step back.

He lumbered onto the roof, dragging his right leg. He elbowed the door shut and waggled his fingers in a gesture of demand. "The book."

Fear surged through her. She moved away, felt a scream erupt. He lunged, clamped a hand over her mouth and clutched her wrist, breath heavy against her face.

Got to get away from him. Get away. She kicked at him, grabbed the fingers that dug into her cheek, forced them back, back, until she heard a snap.

He grunted, dropped his hand.

"Bitch."

She spiraled to pull away, hit the gash on his head with the back of her hand. He winced. Blood trickled into his eye. He swiped at the cut with the back of his hand, smeared blood across his forehead.

Like finger-paint.

She moved out of reach.

He lurched toward her, snarling, seized her arm with his left hand and twisted it.

She struggled, writhing, thrashing through a fog of pain. She kicked and missed and kicked again. She bit his sleeve and spit out the sour-salt taste of the cloth.

She recoiled, and slammed her knee upward between his legs.

He groaned, doubled over, stumbled back. Her leg shot up again, trying for a second kick and he snatched her ankle. She fell onto her back, clutching air.

He dove at her. She rolled onto her side and he crashed into her shoulder, panting.

The Teletype clattered in the shed. He relaxed his grip, rose, and shambled toward the sound. She struggled to her feet.

Block his way.

He smirked as if he had won.

She moved between him and the shed.

He kept coming, growling, dragging his foot, swinging his arm.

She backed away, heartbeat thumping in her ears, heaving in her chest, choking in her throat, too afraid to scream.

A wild howl rose from him.

She inched further back, arms and legs heavy with fear. He circled her, his right hand limp, his left hand flexing.

He lunged at her.

She dodged when he dove forward. He careened against her.

Can't let him stop Torch.

She ran at him, head down, rammed him. Pain jarred through her as her shoulder slammed into his gut.

The impact knocked her off balance. She scrambled to her feet and slammed into him again.

He staggered back, back, arms waving, and disappeared off the edge of the roof.

A cry of terror trailed behind him.

She heard a thud, an animal sound almost like a sigh.

Then silence.

Panting, terrified, she crept to the edge of the roof and peered into the alley. Zaid lay splayed on the cobbles, his head at an odd angle, blood seeping from his nose and gaping mouth.

She froze, unable to move.

This didn't happen.

He looks like a clown in his bloody pantaloons.

No one in the building across the way. Shutters on the windows closed. No one in the alley except Zaid. The only movement, on the balcony opposite, a tag fluttering in the wind that was tied to a propane tank.

A shudder of cold passed through her, rising up her spine. Her teeth began to chatter. Her arms trembled. She crossed them over her chest and grasped her elbows. She pulled tighter, and still her arms quivered.

She pulled back from the edge, her shoulder throbbing, the skin on her arm prickling where Zaid had grazed against it when he hurtled off the roof. She tripped on a clay pot; it toppled over and cracked, spilling dirt along the edge of the roof.

She stumbled against the flagpole, felt it vibrate, metal fasteners ringing against the pole as the flag snapped in the wind.

Got to get away from here, get downstairs.

She crossed the roof to the door and paused at the landing. She thought of Drury, of MacAlistair.

Zaid had killed them. He would have killed me.

She went back to lock the shed and tried to lock the door to the roof. The shattered doorframe blocked the head of the bolt.

The damn door won't close.

She pocketed the keys and hesitated on the landing, exhausted. I killed a man.

"Killed him in battle," she heard Rafi's voice say. "You did what you had to do."

Then she started down the stairs, clutching the banister.

Chapter Thirty-One

Korian stood in the corridor outside her office, sucking on his pipe. "You look awful. What happened?"

"I tripped on the stairs. I think I hurt my shoulder."

Go away, Korian.

"I thought I heard something," he said. "A commotion in the alley behind the Legation."

"I don't know anything about it. I was on the other side of the building."

Korian leaned one elbow against the wall and drew on the pipe, saturating the hallway with his smarmy presence. Lily's eyes began to tear.

He waved the other hand vaguely in the direction of the street. "Something's going on out there."

They found Zaid?

"I don't know anything about it."

Leave me alone, Korian.

Korian leaned toward her. "I wanted to say goodbye."

"I don't leave until tomorrow."

"I'm leaving myself. Got a new appointment. We could have dinner tonight to celebrate."

"I can't."

"Have to wash your hair again?" He raised his head and sniffed. "You certainly keep a clean head of hair."

She tried to duck into her office. "I don't have time." There was no way around him. "Have to pack."

He moved closer. "You still have to eat."

"I have a previous engagement."

Get lost, Korian. And take your pipe with you.

The noise outside became more insistent. She thought she heard Lieutenant Periera's voice argue with the guard at the door. The ruckus echoed through the hallway and grew more strident. She dodged under Korian's arm, feeling the wrench in her shoulder when she straightened up. From behind her desk, she watched Lieutenant Periera and his sergeant march down the hall and burst into Boyle's office. Korian slithered after them and stood right outside the door.

She heard Boyle ask Pereira, "Do you have an appointment?"

"Last night," Periera said in an imperious voice that reverberated through the corridor, "someone killed one of the sentries at Cape Spartel, wounded the other and stole a patrol car."

"How does that concern me?"

"The wounded officer made his way to the lighthouse and contacted us from there."

"I'm sorry to hear that happened. It is not a matter for this office, however, and is no excuse for you to storm in here unannounced."

"I am conducting a serious police investigation. The van was found in the street outside the Legation, and the man was seen entering this building." Lily could hear the impatient slap of Periera's baton against the leg of his trousers. "He fell, or was pushed, from your roof into the alley behind the building."

"You must be mistaken," Boyle said. "The roof is locked. He fell from another building."

Lily moved into the hall and peeked around Korian. She saw Boyle rearrange the pens on his desk, lean back in his chair and contemplate Periera. "No one from the Legation has been to Cape Spartel recently."

"The man appears to be a Riffian."

"Well, then," Boyle spread out his hands, "you have no business here. Check next door or one of the buildings in the alley. Good day, Lieutenant. You know the way out."

"Appearances can be deceiving. I must go to your roof. Then I'll decide what to do."

"No." Boyle picked up one of the pens and began to write on a pad. "You may not."

"You would impede the operation of justice? Your roof may be the scene of a crime."

"The Legation is United States territory," Boyle said without looking up. "You have no jurisdiction here. I will thank you to leave."

Periera lifted his hands to remonstrate. "Colonel Yuste will hear of this."

"I'm sure he will."

Pereira turned on his heel and strode down the hall, signaling his sergeant to follow.

Lily ducked back into her office. Pereira passed Lily's door.

"Five o'clock tomorrow, Miss Sampson," he said without missing a step and continued down the hall.

She watched him swagger out of sight. When he was gone, she strode down to Boyle's office and sank into the chair across from his desk. He waited, his head resting against his left hand, scratching a pen along the pad with his right.

"The roof," she said.

"What about the roof?"

"The door needs to be repaired." She craned her neck to scrutinize the pad. He was doodling.

He turned to a fresh page and scribbled something. "Any other damage?"

"No. Yes. A broken flower pot."

He made another note. "Do I want to know what happened on the roof?"

She took in her breath. "No."

He replaced the pen on the desk, arranged his hands on the blotter and looked across at Lily. "I have some news for you."

"About Suzannah?"

"She left for Fez, has some distant relatives there. Drury left her a small trust fund, but she may not be able to get it until after the duration, when the war is over. I was able to give her some money to tide her over." He looked down at the desk and straightened the pen. "It's your friend Lalla Emily."

"What about her?"

"Lalla Emily, Sheerifa of Ouezzane, is dead."

Lily leaned forward. "How?"

"She died peacefully in her sleep last night," Boyle said. "Her funeral is tomorrow. The Moslems here think of her as a saint, and there's talk of making her tomb a marabout, a holy place of pilgrimage. Also, I have a message for you from Major Pardo."

"A message?" There was one on the Teletype, too. She'd forgotten.

"Your replacement, Warrant Officer Blufield, will arrive Sunday, tomorrow, early afternoon."

"Oh?"

"According to Yuste, you must leave by Monday."

"I'll be ready."

"I made reservations for you at Hotel TransAtlantique in the Ville Nouvelle in Meknes. It's only a few kilometers from Volubilis."

She stood up. "You told me."

"And since you are our current cultural attachée," he raised an eyebrow in emphasis and paused while she took in the new title, "I was able to requisition a jeep for your use."

Boyle stood up and came around the desk. "You know, I was skeptical when you first showed up here."

"You advised me to go to the beach, as I recall."

The message on the Teletype, still unread, nagged at her. From Adam? About Torch? Impatient to leave, she was almost at the door of Boyle's office.

"About Korian," Boyle said before she reached the door.

"What about him? He said he's leaving."

"He's been kicked upstairs. He'll be in charge of his own mission."

"He's being rewarded?"

"We don't like to make a fuss."

"Where is he going?"

"Brazzaville, in French Equatorial Africa."

"Brazzaville?"

"He speaks French."

"It's out of the war zone," Lily said.

"And he'll be better off there. It will be more difficult to feed his little habit. He'll have to find another hobby. Cirrhosis of the liver, maybe."

She backed into the hallway. "I have to go upstairs."

At the entrance to the roof, she paused on the landing, a pulse beating in her ears. Suppose Zaid is still there? Suppose he hadn't died when he fell off the roof?

She opened the door and stepped onto the roof. She listened, edged toward the back and looked down into the alley.

Zaid was gone. Two men from the Guardia Civil stood over a dark stain on the pavement.

She backed away, unlocked the shed, and stared dumbly at the table, staring at the Teletype.

Finally, she pulled the dispatch from the platen. It took only a few minutes to decode it.

"Warrant Officer Blufield of CIC will arrive Tangier Sunday, November 8, at fourteen hundred hours. Give him your recipes for blueberry pies," it read. "Return to station for additional transmission this p.m. at twenty-one hundred hours."

She locked the shed and went back downstairs. She washed and packed. She checked supplies for her survey, making sure everything she would need was ready. Spirit levels, stakes, plumb bobs, surveyor's pins, mason's twine, measuring tape, record forms.

Record forms. She had forgotten record forms.

She found mimeograph stencils in the secretary's office, prepared forms for measurements and architectural features, houses, and burials.

Graph paper! She forgot to buy graph paper. She made a note to stop at a stationer's in Meknes.

She placed the mimeograph stencils on the drums, remembering the smell of ether and alcohol and the cold paper from her early days as a graduate student when she had been a T.A. at the Oriental Institute. Just as it happened then, her hands were smudged with purple stains from the toner.

When she finished, she washed, went back to her room, and fell exhausted across the bed. When she awoke, it was dark.

She had dinner by herself in the wine bar at the El Minzah and returned half an hour before nine o'clock. The night was chilly. She fished a jacket from the top of her suitcase and climbed to the roof.

The door had already been repaired.

The stars were clear and radiant in the night sky; last night's sliver of a crescent moon had disappeared.

Tonight was the dark of the moon.

Chapter Thirty-Two

She unlocked the shed, opened the *Ethnology of the Kwakiutl*, and wrote out the code for November 8. While she waited, she turned on the radio next to the bar, just loud enough to make her feel less alone. The only station working was the French language BBC, where a throaty singer, crooning a song about a lost love, was interrupted. A man's voice intoned, *"Écoutez Yankee Lincoln. Écoutez Yankee Lincoln. Robert arrive. Robert arrive,"* and then the singer continued to mourn his lost love.

At 00:00 Greenwich Mean Time, on the morning of November 8, she received a transmission from Casablanca. Decoded, it read: "The Torch is lit."

The radio still played. *La Mer*. The white noise kept her going.

At 06:17 she transmitted a message from Allied headquarters in Gibraltar to General George S. Patton aboard the *Augusta*, lying off the coast of Casablanca.

"Play ball," it said, the signal for the task force to disembark.

Operation Torch was underway.

At 08:00, the Marine from downstairs came up to the roof to raise the flag.

Once, the radio crackled and a voice in German filtered through the music. *"Achtung—Achtung—Achtung. Ein Americanishes kraftsheer ist auf den nordwest Kuste Africas gelandet."*

She continued working furiously, with hardly enough time to decode one dispatch before encrypting another and sending it off.

Wind began to whip at the pages. She held them down with the heavy ethnography, found cups and saucers on the cupboards in the shed, and used them as paperweights. Anything that worked.

By noon, the back of her neck was stiff, the space between her shoulder blades ached. When the pace of the dispatches slackened a bit she paused, bent her arms at the elbows and rotated them to relieve the tension.

A knock sounded at the door of the roof. She stiffened. The knock sounded again.

What was she afraid of? Zaid was dead, taken away in an ambulance by the Guardia Civil. Periera had left the premises.

She opened the door and found Warrant Officer Blufield on the landing.

"Blufield reporting for duty." He began to salute and hesitated, not sure of what to do.

"Am I glad to see you." Lily waved him onto the roof and started toward the shed. "Sink any ships lately?" She turned back to make sure he followed.

He was right behind her. "The Major really reamed me out for that. But I wasn't talking about Enigma."

"That's the name of the operation at Bletchley Park?"

"No. That's called Ultra. Enigma's the name of the German code."

"You're doing it again."

"Sorry. You won't report me to the Major, will you?" He ducked his head and smiled. "I was thinking of the peacetime applications." The glow of the future still glimmered in his eyes.

"You talk like this to everyone?"

"No, ma'am. Just you, and only because we talked about it before."

"It's a bad habit, Blufield, discussing security matters, with me or anyone else, even people in G2." His face flushed, suffused with embarrassment. He shuffled his feet and looked down, abashed.

"Especially in Tangier," Lily went on. "It's an international community, full of Axis spies. People's lives, the outcome of the war, could be placed in jeopardy."

"I get the message. Casablanca's no better. I've been careful."

"You come from Casablanca? What can you tell me about Torch?"

"Some opposition from the Vichy French. There was a naval battle; they bombarded the *Massachusetts*. The landing force ran into resistance, especially at Port Lyautey. We suffered some casualties. But the French had more. We're beginning to thrust inland. Should clean it up in a week, two at the outside."

Behind her, the Teletype continued to spill out new dispatches. "Time to get back to work. You know the code we use here and the broadcast frequencies?"

He nodded. "I was the one at the other end in Casablanca between midnight and 06:00."

She felt a twinge of disappointment. "I thought it was Major Pardo." She reached into her pocket. "I leave for Meknes this afternoon. Have a few things to do before I go." She held out the keys. "The round one's for the roof; the hexagonal one for the shed. It's easy to remember. 'R' for 'round' stands for roof, 'S' for 'six sides' stands for shed."

"The Major told me to tell you to report to him in Casablanca when you're finished at Volubilis."

She felt color flood her cheeks and was surprised at how much she looked forward to seeing Adam again. She turned to go, hoping Blufield didn't notice. He was already at the Teletype and encrypting the next communication. He worked quickly, able to send and receive messages with remarkable speed.

She left the roof and went downstairs to Boyle's office. "I've come to say goodbye."

He looked up from the paper he was reading. "You look terrible. Better get some rest."

"Can't." She'd had no more than short snatches of sleep in the last forty-eight hours. Her eyes were gritty, but she had to keep moving. "Too much adrenaline."

"The jeep is parked outside. Ask Jessup to help you load it when you're ready."

Suddenly she was hungry. "Going to get something to eat first."

She headed for the last time for the Petit Socco, found a table that overlooked the square and looked over the menu. The thought of food made her queasy. She ordered a poached egg, some toast, and tea.

Tired beyond rest, she sipped the tea—too sweet, too hot, the bright taste of mint suffusing her mouth and nostrils. She stared in a daze at the swirling crush of people funneling through the square and raised the glass of tea in salute to the city of drifting souls—the leftovers of Europe and America—remittance men, black sheep, drunks staggering too early in the day, addicts with blank eyes and lost faces, Berbers who moved among them like medieval conjurers.

Lily would never see Lalla Emily again, would never see Drury nor MacAlistair. Phillipe, Lalla Emily's grandson, had arranged for them to be buried in a small, weed-choked lot across from her villa. Suzannah had already left for Fez. In a month, a few weeks perhaps, Lily would be in Casablanca with Adam.

With the jeep loaded, she drove south, past Chaouen, over the Rif Mountains and past Fez toward Meknes.

She stopped at Volubilis and left the jeep, strolling through the ruins of the triumphal arch, past the forum and its tall columns, still standing, past the basilica where Roman officials once sat in judgment, and down the Decumanus Maximus, past the Roman villas with their mosaic floors barely visible under the dust—where Orpheus charmed wild beasts dancing in an endless round, where Bacchus drove a chariot pulled by panthers, where Venus bathed with her nymphs. This was the house where the bust of the king of the Berbers, Juba II, descendant of Hannibal, was found.

Once, Moroccans, convinced that the site was built in Biblical times by the pharaoh of Egypt, called the site Ksar Faraoun, The Pharaoh's Palace. From here, the wise and kind Juba II ruled the Berber kingdom, Roman procurators ruled Mauretania, and Moulay Idriss, descendant of the Prophet, brought Allah to the Latinized Berbers and Jews and Syrians and established the Sultanate of Morocco.

Lily could see his tomb from here in the holy town of Moulay Idriss, a little more than a mile away. Flat-roofed houses of the town climbed the hills beyond Volubilis, and cascaded through narrow lanes. The tomb of Moulay Idriss and his shrine dominated the elevation between two hills.

She thought of the poster she had seen so long ago in Drury's office that said, "What matters most is how you see yourself." Did Moulay Idriss see himself as the savior of Morocco?

It was getting dark now. She went back to the jeep and wondered how Drury saw himself. In the end, Drury had seen himself as an unconquerable hero, and maybe he was.

She had one foot in the past, in the Roman world where conquerors came into Africa and brought their engineering genius, their villas with mosaic floors, their law courts and Byzantine churches. The past was her reality, with its surge of conqueror after conqueror that fashioned Morocco.

She thought of Blufield, his mind poised on the cusp of the future. Neither of them lived in the present; both lingered on the moving pinnacle of time.

Driving away from Volubilis, she thought she understood.

It was all of a piece.

To receive a free catalog of Poisoned Pen Press titles, please contact us in one of the following ways:

Phone: 1-800-421-3976
Facsimile: 1-480-949-1707
E-mail: info@poisonedpenpress.com
Website: www.poisonedpenpress.com

Poisoned Pen Press
6962 E. First Ave. Ste. 103
Scottsdale, AZ 85251